SHARKEY

SHARKEY

James Wyckoff

DOUBLEDAY & COMPANY, INC.
GARDEN CITY, NEW YORK
1980

All of the characters in this book are fictitious, and any resemblance to actual persons living or dead is purely coincidental

ISBN: 0-385-11564-4
Library of Congress Catalog Card Number 77-76273

FOR

SUSAN

SHARKEY

1

It had been a hard winter and spring had come late to the country, but now summer was there and the land breathed with new life. Now the grass was over four inches and the grazing was good.

This day there had been nothing in the sky other than the bright sun; and in the late afternoon its dying light reached gently across the town, touching the wooden buildings, the dirt streets, the new cattle pens down at the railhead. As evening came lamps were lighted, and a new current entered the atmosphere; the current of expectancy. This was the eighties and Sunshine Basin awaited its first Texas cattle drive.

In a back room of the Star saloon four men sat

around a baize-topped table. A fifth man had just entered. He was tall, bony, in his sixties, with a long nose and somber eyes. The four at the table had their attention fully upon him.

"Well, Clyde?" These words came from a heavy man wearing a clean white stetson hat with a straight, crisp brim.

"He will have at best limited use of his arm. I repeat —at best." Dr. Clyde Hollingsworth paused to allow it to reach them.

"You are saying his gun arm is dead," said a thickly bearded man, as he drummed his fingers on the table.

A long sigh seemed to run through the length of Hollingsworth's body, all the way down to his toes, at the end of which he said, "That's the size of it." His words were addressed to the whole group, but his eyes were on Horace Butterfield, who had spoken the grim summation.

"He's lucky to be alive." Carl Calhoun pushed his white hat onto the back of his head, his forefinger just touching beneath the hard brim. Like his hat, he too was crisp, clean, neat. A man of fifty-some, he owned the New York House, Sunshine Basin's one hotel. And he was the mayor.

Butterfield scratched into his heavy beard as with his other hand he reached for the bottle in front of him. "Boys, another round." And without waiting for a response, he poured, his eyes squinting apparently from the effort. He passed a fresh tumbler to Hollingsworth.

All drank, their faces serious with the gravity of the

situation which they, as the town's leading citizens and town council, now faced.

"Gentlemen, we are in a tight, and that's for sure." This unnecessary addition was brought by a round man with a very white face, a bald head circled by a careful fringe of white hair, and long white hands. Except that Coy O'Donnell, the town's banker, just about never said anything unnecessary without a reason; and as it developed, he was only warming the group into what he really had to say.

"Gentlemen, just to review for a moment. The first herd left the Red River June 1. It will take thirty-five to forty days to move that twenty-five hundred head, figuring on ten to twelve miles a day." He leaned forward, his round belly touching the edge of the table, and placed one long, white hand flat on the green baize table top. His rather large forehead rose into a web of shiny wrinkles as he looked at his companions. "You can figure it out."

"It will be any day now," Carl Calhoun said musingly, and to himself he again counted the New York House's rooms.

The man directly across from Coy O'Donnell had heard something else in the banker's words. He took the cigar out of his mouth quickly. "You mean, like Abilene."

"Carew, I mean like Abilene, and Wichita, and Ellsworth, and Newton, and Dodge, and any other cow town you can name. If we don't learn something by their example, then we don't deserve to have a town." O'Donnell sat back, sniffing loudly against the cigar smoke, his eyes still on the other man, his point made. He wore no hat, yet he perspired easily, and although he had been present at the meeting a good quarter of an hour, the imprint of his hat band was still visible on his damp forehead.

Butterfield said, "We all know where we stand; or do we?" he added, raising his long eyebrows.

"I am not so sure," Coy O'Donnell answered to that, removing his hand from the table top and sitting back. "Except to say we are standing—or better, sitting—on a powder keg."

Calhoun carefully lifted his stetson hat by the crown and settled it more squarely on his head. He let his fingers circle loosely his glass of whiskey as he spoke. "We have got to decide what we want, and how we want to play our hand."

"I told you, I told you," Carew said, sharp, pointing his finger at no one in particular. "This town will go down just like those others. People want the business from the Texans, but they don't want the price." He coughed quickly, almost without a pause, and swept on. "Hell, we do not want the Texas cattle fever; the quarantine's for the whole territory, and that for sure includes Sunshine Basin. I am for enforcing the quarantine."

"Yes, but may I remind you gentlemen of what we have been discussing for days—the town's financial condition." Coy O'Donnell's words fell with a persuasive quiet into the gathering.

"The farmers, the ranchers, don't want the Texas

competition," Carew insisted. "They want to raise their own beeves and sell 'em to the eastern market."

"But the town needs the cattle trade," Calhoun said, "and there is no real proof on the fever hitting northern stock."

"Is there no way out?" asked Butterfield. "I mean, do we have to buy the gunfighting and crazy cowhands?" He raised his glass, then put it down abruptly without drinking, to resume. "Can't we control it? Sure the farmers don't want the Texas cattle, but everyone else does." And he looked coldly at Carew.

Hollingsworth, who had not spoken since his report, had been working his loose mouth vigorously as though trying to find a grape pit before spitting it out; but it was words he was chewing. Now, having got them into the right place, he said to Butterfield, "You mean, you want your beef on the hoof and on the plate too; that it, Horace?" And there was amusement in his deep eyes for a moment.

Calhoun held out his hand to Carew for a cigar. "It is a good bit late to be talking all this over again now, is it not?"

"It is that." Coy O'Donnell leaned forward again and this time he placed both palms flat on the table. "Time has run out, and we have a town with no marshal, or one that is shot up, which is the same, and we're about to have a dollop of Texas drovers on our hands." He raised his hands abruptly from the table and spread his palms wide. "What are we going to do? We want their business, and so we have to play along with them. But we don't want the trouble they bring."

He raised his hands higher and shrugged. "What do we do?" Suddenly he dropped his hands and looked seriously at his companions. "I will tell you; we hire a new marshal. That is what we must do." And he slapped the top of the table smartly and sat back. Reaching into his waistcoat of black broadcloth, he drew forth a large gold watch and looked at the time.

Silence followed this appraisal of the situation, and they all felt its weight.

Hollingsworth appeared to give even a longer sigh this time. And he spoke his words carefully, "You mean, we have got to fire Tanner."

"Did I say that?" Coy O'Donnell shot his eyes to the doctor. "I do not want words put into my mouth, Clyde."

"I took it to be what you meant." Hollingsworth flushed darkly with annoyance at the hairsplitting, and remembered that he didn't like banks.

"Yes," O'Donnell covered quickly, his tone mollifying. "I didn't take you to be previous, Doc."

"The point is taken," Butterfield put in. "We do need a marshal; no matter."

And again there was silence while they turned this over.

Calhoun summed their hesitation. "But who? Who is fast enough, tough enough, and reasonably honest?"

"We'll not get another like Tanner in a jiffy; that's what I know," Carew said. He was the town's bootmaker, but many mistook him for an undertaker. He had that air of finality and gloom about him that is usually associated with the profession.

"The question is," Calhoun said, "who is going to tell Tanner? Eh, gentlemen?" And he looked around at the others with a sour smile on his face.

Butterfield reached and poured, then passed the bottle to Calhoun. "I would not savor the job," he said. He cut his eye quickly to Calhoun. "Perhaps the mayor?" leaving it hang, wry.

"Thank you," Calhoun rejoined grimly. He looked across at Hollingsworth. "What did Tanner say when you told him about his arm?"

Hollingsworth's eyes were tight as he said, "He told me I could go plumb to hell."

This brought a laugh from the group.

In the pause that followed, Coy O'Donnell again looked at his watch. Then his eyes swept the gathering. "Our hesitancy in the face of our problem over cattle, quarantine, and town marshal compels me to remind us of the most important point of business," he said softly. "A point we seem to have overlooked."

He waited.

It was Charlie Carew who finally gave word to the thought that was reaching them. "You mean—Siringo."

In the thick silence that followed this, Coy O'Donnell took out his watch and wound it.

"Yes," he said. "Siringo; the linchpin of our—uh—problem."

It was as though in answer to this that three gunshots were suddenly heard coming from the bar in the next room.

2

Those shots were followed by the door that led to the saloon proper bursting open.

An agitated man with a totally bald head entered swiftly. He was wearing an apron. His hands were wet, for he had just had them in water and had not taken time to dry. Loud voices mixed with raucous laughter came crashing after him from the bar.

"Charlie Earnshaw and a couple Siringo men have took over the saloon. They're talkin' about treeing the town." The bartender's words stumbled out of his tense lips. He ran the back of his wrist across his sweating forehead, and then, remembering his hands were still wet, he began drying them rapidly on his apron.

"Get Tanner . . ." Calhoun started to say, and realized the foolishness of calling on a lawman who was at home in bed with a useless gun arm.

Now a voice called loudly through the open door. "Cyrus, bring out the boys in the back room!" The invitation was followed by more gunfire, and loud laughter.

The group at the table had risen as a man appeared in the doorway. He was a squat individual with a filthy bandanna around his neck and a battered derby hat square on his big head. He brandished a six-gun at the five, a grin going almost all the way across his bearded face.

"Earnshaw, what do you think you are doing?" Calhoun demanded. "You know the law about checking guns."

"Mayor, we are just funning a little. I mean, since the marshal went and killed two of Mr. Siringo's best men." Abruptly, Earnshaw's good humor changed. His words were cold now as he said, "You gents, just come inside and have a little drink with us." He waved the gun to underline the invitation and stood back to allow them to file through the door.

Butterfield said, "The man has got the gun."

"Smart figuring there," Earnshaw said, and the wide grin returned to his hairy face.

There were about twenty customers in the saloon, plus Earnshaw's two companions, Nile Bowdrie and Little John Hendricks. These two were leaning against the bar, facing the room, with their handguns pointed at the subdued customers, most of whom were seated. Not a one of the clientele was drinking.

"Cyrus, serve whiskey to these gentlemen," Earnshaw said to the bald-headed bartender. "It's on the house, so do be generous!" And he and his two comrades broke into loud laughter at this brisk sally.

They were a rough-looking trio. All present in the room respected their swift reflexes. These were the most lethal of Siringo's gunswifts and cowboys; men whom Clay Tanner had ordered out of town a good six months ago.

Cyrus poured, his hand almost steady, though he did get some on the bar.

"Don't spill any!" barked Little John Hendricks. He was indeed short; and with his close eyes and tight mouth he looked anything but friendly. Nile Bowdrie, on the other hand, appeared almost of an amiable disposition, although anyone accepting that as a true interpretation of his character would have been mistaken. Bowdrie, in fact, was no person to mess with. It was claimed that once, piqued by an old saloon swamper who had inadvertently spooked his horse, Bowdrie had set fire to him. The man had recovered, but those who recounted the incident were no longer the same for having witnessed such brutality.

"Earnshaw." Carl Calhoun's voice was level. He was no coward. Nor were the others, but it was also no time for foolish heroics. "You and these men were ordered out of town six months ago by the marshal. What are you doing here!"

The grin broadened on Earnshaw's face as he leaned on the bar; but not for a moment did his pistol waver.

"Sir, you are really funning us boys. Marshal, you

say." He cut his eye quick at his two companions, who picked it up and on the instant the three were again roaring with laughter; though not ever losing their attention to their weapons.

"Marshal, eh?" Earnshaw went on sniffing loudly, and still with a chortle in his voice. "Well, where is the marshal of Sunshine Basin? Back home nursing his clipped wing, is he?" And his chunky frame shook at the thought, while his two companions joined in again.

"Hell," said Nile Bowdrie, "ain't it the marshal we do want to see!"

The three now looked determinedly toward the swinging doors of the saloon, as though expecting Marshal Tanner to appear. But all that entered was the night air.

"Maybe the marshal don't want to see us," said Little John.

"You mean," cried Earnshaw, "you don't mean the marshal of Sunshine Basin don't want to see little old us! He ain't scared of little old us, is he!" And he thundered the last words while his eyes popped in feigned surprise and he pounded his fist onto the top of the bar. Meanwhile the group of five stood there, not drinking, and making no attempt to conceal the disgust they felt.

Earnshaw stopped suddenly, and took them in, as though realizing their attitude for the first time. Then, without the slightest warning, he fired a shot into the floor at Hollingsworth's feet. But Clyde Hollingsworth hadn't been a frontier doctor all those years for nothing. He didn't move, though his face did whiten considerably, while the irises in his eyes came to pin-points, and his jowls started to work.

"Shoot my foot off," he said, "and I won't be able to walk over to pronounce on you after the marshal cold decks you."

This sally was a mistake, for Earnshaw turned red with anger and now raised his six-gun to point it right at Hollingsworth's chest. There was a charged silence while the two men faced each other. The gunman, furi-ous, right on the point of retaliation, and the doctor, just standing there, gripping his courage. To some, and very likely to Hollingsworth, the moment seemed end-less.

There was not a murmur in the saloon. Then, some-one moved his arm and a silver dollar fell off the bar. It landed on the floor on its edge, rolled a few inches, fell flat, wobbled, and was still. All had heard it without moving.

"You wanted to see me?"

Those words, coming from the back of the room, cut into that tableau like a skinning knife.

The three gunmen wheeled.

A tall, broad-shouldered man stood in the open—and forgotten—doorway to the back room. His right arm was in a sling, while crooked in the crotch of his left, and with his forefinger visibly on the trigger, was a dark blue sawed-off shotgun. This wicked-looking weapon with its wide scatter was pointed right at those three toughs who stood at the bar; their laughter now plastered dry all over their faces.

"You are under arrest," Clay Tanner said.

A beat followed.

And then Earnshaw said, with a slight movement of his six-gun, "There is three of us, Tanner."

The mirror behind the bar shattered into a hundred pieces as the blast of the shotgun tore into the room.

The three Siringo men stood frozen, drained of color, while in total silence a brindle cat slowly entered the saloon beneath the batwing doors, looking neither to right nor left.

"Next load of blue whistlers will cut you three right off at the pockets," Clay Tanner said.

Three handguns fell to the floor; there was no need for the marshal to order it.

"We was just playin' a little, Marshal," Earnshaw said carefully, trying to sound easy.

"I am not."

Somebody near the wall sneezed.

"Cyrus, take their guns."

When the bartender had done it, Tanner said, "Now move," pointing the twin holes of that deadly shotgun in the direction of the swinging doors.

Little John Hendricks and Nile Bowdrie stepped away from the bar, but Earnshaw was slower.

"I am reading it right along with you, Earnshaw," Tanner said. "Don't try it." And he motioned him to move close to his companions.

The marshal had just spoken when the batwing doors of the saloon swung open suddenly and a big man wearing a dusty black stetson hat and a faded hickory shirt entered. All heads turned in the direction of this unexpected visitor. No one had ever seen him before.

"You come at a bad time, stranger," Tanner said, while the visitor's quick step away from the line of fire did not escape him. He was real fast, though clearly no longer a young man.

"Just passing through, Marshal. Didn't figure to interrupt your party."

Tanner motioned to the Siringo men to move faster. They were almost at the batwing doors when a large piece of glass suddenly fell out of the broken mirror and crashed onto the row of bottles behind the bar. The brindle cat, who had been sitting there, let out a screech and jumped in Tanner's direction. In that split moment Earnshaw grabbed the stranger and stepped behind him, using him as a shield, while his hand streaked to a hideout weapon under his shirt.

But that stranger was quicker. With one stroke he ducked, drove his elbow deep into the pit of the gunman's belly, doubling him; then wheeled and brought his right forearm down like a singletree on the back of Earnshaw's neck. The gunman fell as though poleaxed. Almost without pause, in the same flowing movement, the visitor, whom nobody had ever seen before, kicked the hideout gun to Tanner's feet. Then he rubbed his nose with his fist, took off his hat, and replaced it on his big gray head, his light blue eyes resting on the marshal's wounded arm. The marshal nodded to Bowdrie and Hendricks. "Pick him up."

As the party carrying the unconscious Earnshaw

reached the doorway, Tanner said, "Cyrus will give you a drink on me, stranger."

The big man grinned. "I do appreciate it, Marshal."

"I am beholden," said Tanner. "Cyrus, make it all he wants." Then, to the stranger, "You got a handle, mister?"

That grin spread all over the stubbled face now. "The name is Sharkey, Marshal. Clarence Sharkey."

In the new silence that now fell, Doc Hollingsworth's forehead lifted as he let a soft whistle fall through his lips.

3

As the steel rails of the Santa Fe pushed across the prairie they gave birth to a series of railhead towns. These became the background for those fabled actions wherein the legend of the cowboy, the outlaw, and the lawman was grown. Such rendezvous as Dodge City, Wichita, Abilene, Newton, Caldwell, and Ellsworth sprang up overnight as the great cattle drives poured up the Chisholm Trail from Texas. And with the longhorns came the cowboys—dirty, ornery, full of riproaring fun and money to burn. But there also came the gunmen and tinhorns and the petty thieves and toughs.

By the middle eighties most of the cow towns had

established law and order—courtesy of such as Wild Bill Hickok, Green River Tom Smith, Bat Masterson, Bill Tilghman, Luke Short, Wyatt Earp, and a cadre of other lethal lawmen; and, in result, the dispossessed toughs drifted to other pastures more lucrative.

One of their choices was Sunshine Basin. In response, the Basin's leading citizens had imported a peace officer from Wichita. Only neither he nor those who followed him managed to die of old age. Each one's tenure in the marshal's office was noted for its brevity. The present marshal of Sunshine Basin had been in office eight months—the record.

Clay Tanner had cleaned up the Basin and environs with a dispatch that had staggered all who bore witness. Those toughs who had not died from bullets had been banished beyond the town's limits. Even Siringo, chieftain of the KT spread and its crew of hard-drinking, hard-riding, and swift-shooting cowboys, had been forced to play it close to the vest. For sure, Siringo was biding his time until the longhorns and Texas drovers arrived and the town would have to loosen its grip on law and order. Everyone knew he aimed to move in again on the gambling and dance halls the minute the drive hit town.

The marshal knew it better than anyone else. Two times now they had called him; the first, an attempt to dry-gulch him out at Horn Miller's spread had resulted in two Siringo men in the Basin's Boot Hill, and the arm of the law done in; and the second, while failing again at the Star, simply showed that Siringo was not planning to just sit around and wait.

Clay Tanner was reflecting on all this in his office the morning following the adventure in the Star when there was a knock on the door. It was the stranger, the man called Sharkey who walked in.

Tanner nodded. He was seated at his desk, his hat on.

"Mornin', Marshal."

"Sit," Tanner said, and nodded to a chair with no back.

Smiling broadly at the careful hospitality, Sharkey pulled the chair closer with his foot and sat down.

All the time Tanner kept his eyes close on him. For there was something about the man; he couldn't place it, but something. He knew the name, sure, but there was something else. Something familiar? And it wasn't the picture on his desk, the flyer that had just come from Cheyenne. They had never met, that was for sure, and he had never seen the man before. He looked again at the flyer, comparing the picture to the man now seated in front of him.

"That picture don't do me justice, Marshal," Sharkey said, his smile broadening. "They took it when I was in difficulty, having just spent twenty-four hours lying in a swamp with all them lawmen shooting bullets at me. I mean that was fifteen years back, up to Medicine Bow." And he chuckled deep in his chest. "Fact, I am surprised you could even see a likeness."

Sharkey. How often he had heard that name. A name from the past, a legend; from the old days. Yes, it was him. No doubt. Gray now. Heavier, and lined in the face. In his fifties at least, or could be sixty. Hard to tell. But straight. He sat and stood easy, and he moved fast; testimony bore that in the doings last night. He was also hard as a gun barrel. Not a man to get previous with. Prison sure kept a man fit if it didn't kill him.

"What are you doing in Sunshine Basin?" Tanner asked, squinting at the older man as he reached to his shirt pocket for his makings.

"I am free," Sharkey said. "I done my fifteen years, every minute. You have got no call on me, Marshal." And he too reached to the pocket of his faded hickory shirt and took out his tobacco sack and papers. Though he spoke firm, he was all good humor. No bitterness at all. But Tanner would never forget how he had handled Charlie Earnshaw.

"That is what I know," Clay Tanner said. "Exceptin', if you were just passing through that would be one thing. I am wondering what you might have in mind."

"That your business, son?" The words came sharp, but they were not unfriendly; there was still the smile, while the light blue eyes were straight on Tanner.

Tanner did not like being called "son." He was nigh thirty, and sure enough junior to the older man sitting there in that smelly shirt and filthy black stetson hat, but he was not one to be called "son."

His eyes dropped again to the flyer. "Age about sixty," he read aloud. "You don't look it," he said, his eyes still on the picture; and then looking up suddenly at Sharkey, hoping to catch him off guard. But that man was right there.

"Meaning?" Sharkey had deftly built his smoke and

now struck a wooden match on his thumbnail, one-handed, and lighted it.

"I mean you look some good bit younger. Not that it matters."

"No, it don't matter. But I do look my age. And I am my age, for the matter of that. It's others that looks old for their age, not me who looks young." And he let his left eyelid close slowly while the right eye remained wide open, and a smile touched the corners of his mouth.

"I aim to keep the peace in Sunshine Basin," Clay Tanner said, coming down hard on the words. "I know you had dealings with Siringo in the past. Could be you have come back to the Basin for just that."

He kept his eyes tight on Sharkey, who didn't seem to mind in the least. He just sat there, smoking, cool as a plate of spring water, not at all defensive in the face of the law. It was, Tanner suddenly realized, almost as though that old man was trying to humor him.

A deep chuckle seemed to fill Sharkey's chest, and he ran his palm across his big face a couple of times, smiling.

"Old Siringo's still up to his old ways, I can see from last night. Well, I will tell you, Marshal, I don't give a damn about Siringo. I know he is big in this here part of the country, and I sure don't envy you what with him on the one side and them crazy cowboys from Texas on the other." He chuckled aloud. "Plus the town. Course, the town always wants it both ways. But I have come here on other business."

"Which is?"

The smile came back to the corners of Sharkey's mouth. It broadened slowly and then all at once his whole grainy face broke into a grin. "Son, I do like the way you crowd a man. I see you got the makings of a real good lawman."

Tanner did not like this, but he could hold his own: he was no less tough than that elderly desperado seated before him, and he was patient, too. "I asked you a question, mister."

Sharkey let his grin go easy, as he reached again to his shirt pocket. "I am after horseflesh," he said.

"Wrangling?"

"Here is my contract." And he took out a folded piece of paper from his pocket and placed it on the desk in front of Tanner.

It was a contract all right, and from the Army. Tanner tossed it back. "Maybe you don't know that Siringo has all the wild horse stuff sewed up, and I reckon you know how he is about interference."

"Reckon then Mr. Siringo will have to learn how to share the wealth," Sharkey said, speaking softly all of a sudden. "I have got my contract."

"And Siringo has enough riders to tree this town and half the territory." Tanner almost bit the words. "Looky here, I do not want gunplay. This town is trying to grow, not get itself buried."

"And I am aimin' to make my stake with them horses," Sharkey said. "I have planned it this good while, this real good while, my stake; and not Siringo or the whole of this here territory is not going to stop me." He took the contract and held it up, waving it a little. "This here is my stake."

Clay Tanner leaned back in his chair and looked at the man before him from under the low brim of his hat. Then he leaned forward on the desk, his eyes cold as he looked right into Sharkey's face.

"I am saying one thing. You could be trouble. With Siringo and them horses; and for all I know maybe something from the past. Or even with some punk around here knows who you used to be and wants to build himself a reputation."

"And I will tell you one thing, young feller," Sharkey said, and he got up from his chair and stood real hard and big in front of the marshal and his desk. "And it is this. I will not be looking for trouble. But if trouble comes I want you to know that Sharkey will not be standing there just picking his nose."

He looked down at Tanner, who returned his look in the same way.

"Just do not forget there is the law in Sunshine Basin," Tanner said, "and I am the marshal."

Sharkey had walked to the door. He turned back with his hand on the knob. "And, son, don't you forget it neither." And he walked out.

All Clay Tanner could do was cuss.

4

He sat there—smoking, turning it over. It always comes in bunches, he thought. Well, he would handle it. Or—not. Whichever.

Suddenly he pushed back his chair and was on his feet, reaching for the shotgun lying on the desk. And a wave of sickening frustration hit him as he saw how slow, how awkward he was taking the weapon. He hefted it now in his left hand, feeling for the trigger. All very well, he told himself, when he had time to throw down on a party, like last night, but how would it be to go up against a fast draw? And how about reloading? He knew the answer to both of that.

He stood looking at himself in the cracked mirror

over the washstand, not seeing his features, rather seeing inside to his no-good arm, his no-deputies, his dilemma in the face of the Texans, Siringo, and now—Sharkey.

He stepped away from the mirror fast and snatched up the Greener. And almost dropped it. "Goddamn!"

He sat down, swearing again, and then found himself pondering on the man who had once been the scourge of the law in that whole part of the country. What was it that had struck him so at sight of Sharkey? He had never put eyes on the man in his whole life. And yet, there was the taste of someone familiar.

Oh, he had heard plenty; as who hadn't? From his earliest years the name Sharkey had been the folklore. In school they had played at outlaws and lawmen, and Sharkey had always been more hero than villain. They had all wanted to be Sharkey. Yet, they had never seen him; though he was part of the country—no question. One boy, Todd Mooney, claimed to have seen the great outlaw, over to Medicine Bow; but they only half-believed him, listening to the story of that great moment when Todd had seen Sharkey riding into town with two men, fast, drawing up to the saloon and swinging to the ground real fast. And as the story was retold, the details grew so that after a while it was a whole drama.

And then one day the news came that Sharkey had been taken by a posse of marshals over to Medicine Bow. And that strange moment when having just come home from school he had asked his mother about

Sharkey. She had been standing in the kitchen, poking at the range as he brought in an armful of firewood.

"Clay, you have been crossing the sticks in the wood box again. I ran out of kindling this morning."

"Here is more."

"Yes—now. But I needed it when I needed it."

He mumbled something, always struck by her directness.

"That kind of behavior is lying," she told him. And even now all these years later he could remember her smell, the way she brushed her brown hair from her forehead, the easy, simple way she moved and spoke.

"I know," he said.

"Someday you will have children, you will be a father. I hope you will not teach them that." And he remembered her look on him; not sad, not reproving, not smiling; just her look. It was like a touch.

After a moment, he said, "Did Paw ever tell lies?"

He seldom asked anymore about his father, whom he had never seen; but now he did, even knowing that there was something in her that would not wish to answer; he did not know why.

His mother busied herself for a moment or two with the fire. "Lies?" The word came soft over her shoulder. "Well, not so's you'd really say it like that, I guess." She paused, and he had that funny feeling. Then, in a different voice, "No, I'd say Tom Tanner was an honest man. You could be like him." And quickly, "Are you hungry?"

But he had not finished. Somehow, he had found the

courage to be bolder. "Maw, did you or Paw ever see Sharkey?"

"Who?"

"Sharkey. Maybe you saw him when you lived in Medicine Bow."

"You mean—that outlaw?"

And yes, he reflected now as he sat in his office all the years later, it was that. It was just that. For she knew very well who Sharkey was. She must have. And so why had she been—evasive?

"Did you ever see him?" he had insisted.

She had faced him then, firm, the color rising a little in her cheeks. "Clay, neither your father nor I associated with men like that."

"But . . ."

"I do not want to hear that name again, Clay Tanner." She turned her back on him then and lifted the stove lid and fed wood to the fire. "It is getting late," she went on. "And you must be hungry."

He had always felt that strangeness, the feeling that there was something mysterious about his father, who had been thrown from a wagon box and died of a broken neck just before he was born. That was in Medicine Bow, his mother had told him; after which she had brought her son to Sunshine Basin.

He had not mentioned Sharkey again to her, and she seldom spoke of his father, only pointing him out once in a while as a model for behavior.

After Sharkey's capture he and the other kids had continued to play "Sharkey," but the zest was gone. People still remembered Sharkey, talked about him, telling wild stories. He was "Old Sharkey" then, and although he was locked up in Laramie it was as if he were dead.

And so Tanner had grown up and had gone to cowboying, first with Burns and Wolcott, then a good bit later with Siringo and the KT. And when Siringo had come to him and suggested he take the marshal's job—the former marshal having died of, as the saying went, lead poisoning—he had accepted.

It was one of Siringo's rare mistakes. He must have assumed that Tanner, being quiet, easygoing, and hard-working, could be handled. This mistake he had well rued when Horn Miller's homestead became an issue.

Horn had also been a KT cowhand, older than Clay by a good bit, yet a friend. Like so many hands of the demanding Mr. Siringo, Horn had been encouraged to file on a section of land and prove up on it within the allotted two years, then sell it back to the KT. It was a legal way of increasing KT holdings, and a number of cowboys had gone along with it, in the face of not only ready cash but, more important, the imposing figure of Siringo. Except that Horn had refused to sell. And the new marshal of Sunshine Basin had sided him.

"He is with the law," Tanner had told Siringo at the confrontation.

"Not by my book he isn't."

"Your book is finished," Tanner said. "The old days are gone."

"That man is not going to get away with it."

"He has got away with it, and I am siding him."

"I see," Siringo said, seeing the mistake he had made.

A week later Horn Miller was found lying in a clump of willows at Honey Creek. There was a neat round hole between his shoulder blades.

"I will find the killer," Tanner promised Siringo.

"Good luck."

"It will not be luck."

And he made the promise to Annie and Tom Miller. That had been a good six months ago and Siringo was still trying to get Horn Miller's children off the land.

Tanner had just wound his watch and was thinking it would be time to make his rounds when he heard the boots on the boardwalk outside.

It was Calhoun, Butterfield, and O'Donnell. They entered quietly, with a trace of unease, which showed in the mayor's rapid blinking, in Butterfield's sniffing, and O'Donnell's feeling his gold watch chain; all of it swiftly observed by the marshal.

"Well, gentlemen . . ." Tanner allowed a frosty smile to touch his lips. "Three of you." And he raised his forehead questioningly. "It must be important."

They stood before him while he continued to sit. Calhoun sat down on the backless chair that Sharkey had used, and Tanner nodded to two wooden crates in a corner of the room. "About the best there is, gentlemen. We are short on furniture here."

"We should get to the point," Calhoun said, as the others sat. "Clay, we are concerned about the situation in the Basin since you . . ."

But he let them get no further. Tanner's words were

as cold as his eyes as he said, "And who do you gentlemen have in mind?"

He watched it rock them.

O'Donnell rallied first. "Always did appreciate how you drive the nail, Tanner," he said genially. And the others laughed along with him.

But Tanner's face was straight as a board fence.

"Fact is," Calhoun put it, "we were not actually thinking of that. We wanted to talk to you first."

"I am not interested in talk. I have got my shotgun and I have got my brains and my guts. If you do not like the way I run this here office, then say so. Otherwise, I got work to do."

They exchanged looks, not very easily, for they did not like what they had come to speak about.

"We are sorry," said Butterfield, speaking for the first time. "I know that is not much. And we know what Sunshine Basin owes you . . ."

Tanner was on his feet. The movement sent a twinge of pain to his arm, but nothing showed on his face.

Calhoun held up a hand, as though in restraint. "Clay, there is the town to think about. Hell, man, you can't use your shooting arm. It don't matter how many deputies we sign on, you've still got to be able to operate."

Tanner looked steadily at them for a long moment, while the words the mayor had spoken sank into the room.

At last he said, "You got a good man to put in office, I will step down. But I know you have got nobody. I know you cannot even get deputies, because I have been trying. Nobody wants this job—not with the cattle coming and for sure not with Siringo about to move in. So what the hell are you talking about! You can't replace me. Because there is no one. You know that! So instead of fighting me . . ." He paused and a strange smile came into his face. "Instead of hindering me, why don't you three gentlemen sign on as deputies?"

He let that sink and then he said, "Good day, gentlemen."

And he waited without any further words while his visitors departed.

He waited, looking down at the desk. Then he picked up the shotgun, hefted it, again feeling its balance. "The hell you say," he said aloud. And realizing he was talking to himself, he smiled grimly. That grim smile was still on his face as he stepped out into the street.

The sunlight had moved away from the town now and its rays were on the edge of a lone cloud far to the west. Soon it would be dark, and there was the smell of the prairie night already in the air.

It did not take him long to make his rounds. He was not one to tarry. He had too much self-respect to squander himself. There were a number who spoke to him, admiring how he had handled the Siringo men, but he paid little mind to such idle talk. A couple or three he replied to by asking would they be deputies, but there was no response. There were a lot of eyes on his sling, and he could feel the unspoken thought: what would have happened if that stranger hadn't appeared to buffalo Charlie Earnshaw? But Clay Tanner did not linger on the thought. He had a bigger thought to concern him. More likely sooner than later Siringo would be riding into the Basin for his three men in the town jail.

Tanner had just finished with his rounds and was crossing Main Street to the office when he first heard and then saw the horse and rider. His finger found the trigger of the shotgun as the horsebacker came at the gallop, stirring a great plume of dust, to the consternation of those in the street. It was Hank McAuliffe who drew rein before the marshal: a lean man with red-streaked eyes, for he'd had a long, hard ride.

"Fahnstock herd has crossed the Powder," he said, speaking the words through the dust that clogged his lips. "Got it from Heavy Henderson, who whipped the stage into Amityville. About twenty-five hundred head."

Tanner nodded, feeling his eyes tighten as he looked at the sun, which was just at the end of the day, its rays long on the softening buildings, the settling dust, and the lathered dun horse.

"Good enough," he said. And he added, his eyes on the sweating horse, "I be needin' deputies, Hank."

McAuliffe's red eyes looked away. "Clay, I'd sure like to oblige . . ."

Tanner was already walking away.

In his office he checked the loads of the weapons in the gun cabinet; then he wound the clock. He took up the Greener and walked back out into the street. He needed deputies, and he needed them right now.

5

       He was an older man now and he was tired. He lay on the bed in the little room at the New York House, staring up at the big stain on the ceiling, and at the peeling wallpaper where it met the corner of the room. It was hot, and he had the window wide open. Soon it would be cool, but now it was hot. And so he lay there with nothing moving other than his pulse and his thoughts.

       It was all right lying there, it was good. He could just let his tiredness circulate through his whole body. Yes, even his thoughts were tired. He watched the curtain at the window, hanging limp in the heat of the late afternoon.

It had been a long ride from Laramie. And strange. Not at all what he had imagined in his anticipation. Funny how much he remembered, how much forgotten. The smells, the taste of the high air, the tall sky drawing him and at the same time enclosing him so that he felt one with it and with the earth on which he rode. And at night the breathing of the ground beneath him as he lay in his bedroll or sat at his fire. All that had touched him in a way that he had almost forgotten. Fifteen years! At last the freedom for which all those years he had longed. Even here in the tiny room he could feel free; he was free. And in a certain way he had to tell himself that; that he was really free.

To be free! Oh, God, yes. Was it not this that men fought for? Or said they did. To be free—with no fences, nothing holding you. To come and go as you felt like it. Yes—like the Indians. Except, for them not any longer. They too had been hobbled, stuck on the reservations. And now with the country fenced, and the law all over the place, where could a man go? Well, it was free for him, all the same. Anything was freer than Laramie. That holding, that captivity—he could not ever stand that again. He would not. Never. He had stood it those fifteen years. But no more. Never.

His thoughts turned now to the boy and young woman he had met on his way into Sunshine Basin. That too had surely been strange. Only yesterday it had been, and it was still new in his thoughts.

It was around the middle of the forenoon when he had topped that ridge and for the first time in so long looked down on Sunshine Basin far below, with the river winding through, and on out to the lower country. He had sat his horse awhile then in the shadow of the big butte.

It had been quiet in that big shadow, he recollected now, lying in his room, and he had wondered then on how the town might have changed. For it would have changed. They had told him back at Laramie that there would be changes. Not that he needed their words on it. Would there be anyone there to know him? More than likely not, he had figured. His stamping ground had been more around Shoshone and Medicine Bow.

It had been a truly bright day, the sky cut like metal over the high mountain peaks which were capped with snow even though it was July and time for the first haying. Well, you can still see pretty good, he had told himself, his lips moving with the words.

And those sharp eyes, which had so often studied the trail, or looked cold into another man's eyes, or peered through acrid gunsmoke, now caught the glint of sunlight on metal . . .

And he was out of that saddle—and right now!—as the bullet spanged off rock and went singing into the long valley. And he was rolling over sagebrush and rocks, over the lip of the draw, tugging for air, at last pulling up hard behind a cottonwood tree, his breath sawing. While he had just then noticed the Deane & Adams in his hand, which he must have automatically yanked from his belt—having no holster—as he dove to the earth for safety. By God, he was still handy. Yet he could hardly think the words for he had the urge to vomit, feeling too as though he must have busted something in his insides.

"It is no joke being sixty going on seventy," he had told the warden at Laramie when they had parted company.

Behind the cottonwood, his face pressed to the hard ground, he waited, in glaring sunlight. His chest was still heaving, his legs shook; he kept his lips close together so there would be no noise to his breathing. Be still, he had told himself. Listen. But he could hear only himself.

In the sky above, nothing moved. Now as he grew calmer he began to hear the trees. The bay horse had spooked, but raising his head carefully, he could see him. He was standing not very far away, still wary, with his long ears moving about as he tried to locate sign.

He waited, hearing better as his body grew quieter. Who had shot at him? Who in hell after all these years would try to bushwhack him? Who would have even known he was coming to Sunshine Basin? He had not said it anywhere. After fifteen years who was there left, especially with vengeance? Siringo?

He was able now to relax more, sinking into the ground. He was good at waiting. Even before Laramie he had been good at it, for patience was part of the trail. Only forget Laramie, he told himself. To think about things always brought trouble. You had to be right here, you couldn't be dreaming about some damn thing that was over and done with. That way you invited bullets.

But who? Who was trying to dry-gulch him? Ah, but no—he caught himself; not who, for that led to thoughts. Not who, but where. Where was the bastard? Damn! He must make himself be sharp!

Thus he tried to return to how he had once been— only yesterday—behind the cottonwood while waiting for his would-be killer to appear. Now in the room in town he remembered how it had felt, with the hard ground beneath him and the cutting smell of sage in his face, and the heat of the high sun drilling into his back.

Suddenly, from the side of his vision, without turning his head for fear of giving his position away, he had seen the jay fly up from a clump of young pine. Oh, he would have given plenty for a rifle. He had turned his head slowly to see if he could catch the movement of the person in that stand of pine.

A shot rang out all at once. The bay let out a scream and stumbled. Damn it to hell!

Still, he had remained. For at that distance, and himself without a rifle, he had no chance. He waited while the bay died, with the sun boring down and the sweat pouring into his eyes.

That sun was almost directly overhead when at long last he saw a branch move; a short man stepped out of the timber, apparently satisfied that his quarry was done for, and he was safe. His back was turned, and so his face was not visible, but he appeared hesitant, as he stood looking down at the dead horse. In his hand he held a Winchester with a beat-up stock.

Behind the cottonwood Sharkey had waited. It was a

distance to the other, and he had to be sure. A lot of years had passed since he had measured another man's firepower. And so he waited. Until the other suddenly turned. And it was a boy! He wore a cap with a large peak, and he wore it straight on top of his head, which was covered with a great bush of yellow hair. A kid!

Still, he had waited. Not for nothing had he been top gun all those years in that part of the country. Not for nothing had he survived all the years he had. Nor would he forget his caution now. But at last he was satisfied that the boy must be alone. And so he raised himself carefully, and stood.

"Do not move!" he said to the boy's back.

He watched the other's shoulders freeze.

Now he stepped from behind the cottonwood. "Drop the Winchester."

The rifle fell at the boy's feet.

"The gun belt. Easy."

He could tell the boy's hands were shaking even though he could not see them, as he undid the gun belt and let it fall.

"Walk five paces forward and stay."

After he had picked up the Winchester and belt he studied the sun for a moment, and then said, "Take two more steps and then turn around."

The sun was right in the boy's face as he turned to look at the man. He was also on lower ground, as Sharkey had planned it. He was young, maybe thirteen. He was scared, but Sharkey noted how he was holding onto himself.

"Where is your horse?"

"Don't have a horse. I mean, he's back in the corral."

"Corral?"

The boy realized he had made a mistake and he clamped his jaws tight shut.

"Sonny, you killed my horse, and you came close to killing me."

The boy took a deep breath. He was scared all right. "You be on our land. I was trying to scare you off."

"And my pony?"

"I didn't mean to." And he added, "You can believe it or not."

"You are some helluva shot, young feller."

"Mebbe." The boy was rocking a little on his feet; slight but wiry, his blue eyes wide in his wide face. He started to put his hands in his pockets, but didn't. Then he said, "You be on our land. We want you to get off. My sister told Siringo . . ."

"Siringo . . ."

A puzzled look took over the boy's face. "You ride for Siringo, don't you?"

"Young feller, you got guts or dumbness, I do not know which." Sharkey paused. "I could've shot you right outta that clump of pine. You make more noise just breathing than a cavvy of spooked horses. How come you have lived so long?"

But the boy was dead serious. "Then how come you didn't?" And his eyes went to the Deane & Adams in Sharkey's belt.

Something like a smile started on Sharkey's face, hardly showing in his stubble of beard, he knew, but he could feel it all right. Slowly he took the Deane &

Adams out of his belt and pointed it right at the boy, whose face was suddenly drained of color.

A long moment passed, while Sharkey watched the boy, his finger on the trigger. The boy's right leg began to shake, but his eyes did not falter. By God, Sharkey thought, by God.

"That is why," Sharkey said suddenly, and when he pulled the trigger the click of the hammer on the empty chamber was louder than any pistol shot.

Both the boy's legs were shaking now, but he stood as firm as he could while biting his lip.

"What do they call you, son?"

"Tom. Tom Miller."

"Good enough. Then strip the bay and we'll head for your outfit. Who you got there?"

"Just me and my sister."

Sharkey spent a moment with that, testing it for sincerity, and was satisfied. "Good enough," he said again.

Lying on his bed now he smiled as he thought of Annie Miller. She was a pretty one for sure—about twenty-five or so, he figured—and he had always admired good-looking girls.

She and Tom had told him about Siringo and their father; and the harassing by Siringo's men. And he had learned too that they were good friends of the marshal, Clay Tanner.

Suddenly Annie Miller had said to him, "Mr. Sharkey, we could use a hand here on the ranch, and if you would think of it, it would be a place for you to stay."

Sharkey had liked that. She was direct; he liked that.

He smiled at her. "I'd sure enough like to consider it, ma'am, but I got me a job to do in town."

"Couldn't you do both?" the boy asked.

Sharkey chuckled. "For a raspy young feller who tried to shoot me out of the territory you sure have got a changeable mind."

But no. No, he had his thing to do. Maybe it would have been nice to stay, he reflected now as he lay in his bed, but he wouldn't have lasted. He was not the type for the farm life. Never had been.

But the big event was when he had walked into the Star and seen who the marshal actually was. Funny how he had known it right off. Known it the way he moved. Tanner. He wondered where she'd gotten the name. And he remembered hearing in Laramie news of her moving to Sunshine Basin after Medicine Bow.

But he had not come to the Basin for that. Or had he?

"I am going to make my stake," Sharkey said aloud as he stared at the spot on the ceiling. Yes, he had come to the Basin to make his stake. Too bad if certain people were about. It would not stop him. He had it all figured. Had he not spent days, hours, on it? Years!

"I am going to live my last years decent," he said, again speaking it aloud.

But there was a small voice somewhere inside him asking was that the only reason he had come back to this part of the country.

The bed springs creaked loudly as he shifted his weight. He lay still, listening to the sounds in the street below. It was dark now, and a pale glimmer of light was on the window sill. A dog barked. Then another answered. He heard two men laughing. He found his thoughts again on the Millers. Funny, how they knew Tanner.

He had just started to doze off when a step in the hall outside brought him wide awake. And at once he was on his feet. Just as the knock came at the door.

He stood there, absolutely still, fully aware that the Deane & Adams had no bullets as his hand reached for it even so.

"Sharkey!" The voice was hard, insistent, but low.

In the weak light coming through the window behind him, he watched the doorknob turn, but he had locked the door when he had come in.

He was just going to demand who was there when he heard a sound at his back. Spinning, he saw the legs coming down from the window of the room above. He was across the room and had slammed the barrel of the .44 against the intruder's shin followed by a second stroke into his groin. The man let go a scream of pain and, losing his grip, fell like a sack to the street below. Behind Sharkey there was a crash as the door burst open.

Three men carried him to the floor, but not before he had delivered some damage with the gun barrel. A tremendous blow in the pit of his stomach knocked his breath out; and he was on his back on the floor, with someone's knee against his throat and a knife point at his ear.

"Now you listen, Sharkey. And get this good. You are not wanted in Sunshine Basin."

Although he could barely see the shape of his assailants he could smell them all right. They were liquored well. The speaker leaned real close. "You got that, you old sonofabitch!"

Sharkey could say nothing; there seemed to be no breath in him at all.

"You got that!" And the knife point pushed hard against his neck.

He managed to say, "I got it. Tell Siringo I got it."

"You be shut of this town comes tomorrow sunup."

Suddenly a light went on in a building across the street and he glimpsed the man who had spoken—mustache, scar on one cheek, the reek of 40-rod whistling through dark teeth.

"I got you," Sharkey said after they had gone, and he continued to lie in a heap on the floor. "I will not forget you."

After a while—he did not know how long it was—he realized his ribs were not broken, and save for some cuts and bruises he was more or less intact. Only thing was he felt as though he had been tromped by a bronc.

At last he pulled himself up onto the bed. He lay there a long time until he remembered the .44. But it was gone. And so he was without any weapon at all. As a long while later the sky began to lighten and he felt himself getting mad.

The first rays of the morning sun were just touching into the valley as Sharkey stepped out into the street. He was whistling softly to himself between his teeth. Right then he spotted the two loungers squatting in the doorway of the Pastime directly across from the New York House.

"Well, I will for sure be gone by sunup," he said to himself as he walked toward the livery barn. And he was even madder than when he'd lain in his bed in the very early morning.

6

First there were the mountain men and the trappers, and then came the gold seekers and the buffalo hunters. And then the cattlemen. To the cattleman the cow was the way of life, as the buffalo was for the Indian. The cow offered meat, soap, fat, and candlelight; its skin became a man's clothing, frequently his shelter, the cover for his wagon bows, the rugs in his dwelling. And it provided rawhide for chairs, beds, trunks, baskets, and dough pans. Horses were hobbled with rawhide, and sometimes they had been shod with it; in early days it took the place of iron and wood. The riata had been made of rawhide, and often so were blackboards, slates, playing cards, the tops of faro tables. The cow, if not sacred like the buffalo was for the traditional red man, was still most assuredly the staff of life of the Westerner, and had been especially so for the early Texan; or Texian, as the citizens of the new Republic of Texas had liked to be called. The present Texans weren't all that much different.

One of these was Siringo. Though he had spent the majority of his years away from the Panhandle, building his empire in the Powder River country, Siringo had always been "a Texan." Nobody knew any otherwise, as the saying went.

He had first trail-herded north with his father, who was now a part of the folklore, had fought the Comanche and Kiowa, and the Sioux. There was not much Siringo hadn't been a part of. And from the moment he rode into the Powder River country he had known this was the place for him to build his brand.

The Indians had not agreed with him; and later the outlaws, various cattlemen, and the law offered opposing views. None of it deterred Siringo. He had dealt with all of these elements in his own way—with force and guile. But civilization was encroaching. The West was changing. And Siringo found his world challenged in a way that was difficult to deal with; for while he was a shrewd man, he was not subtle.

There were these damn farmers and homesteaders, the sodbusters. A stupid law it was, the Homestead Act. But he had found his way around it. Stake a fiddle-foot cowboy and he'd prove up on a section of land and sell it back to you.

Excepting he had run into Horn Miller, who for

some damn reason had refused to sell. Gone back on
his agreement, by God. Well, you did not do such a
thing to Siringo. So, tough for Horn. A lesson there for
the rest of the sodbusters and anyone else not to cross
the man who had built what he had. Tough for Horn,
and tough for his kids. Horn had double-crossed him
and he had, by God, paid for it. That was the way it
was. And neatly done too. And the marshal could find
nothing to prove on anything even close to himself. Of
course, he should never have trusted Horn, and for sure
not Clay Tanner.

But now those two Miller kids—the girl and her
brother. He had to go easy there. People got soft when
you dealt with women and children. That last time
Earnshaw and the boys had ridden through the Miller
spread liquored and pop-shooting their guns all over
the place, he had lit into them. It was the wrong way.
Clever was needed there, not muscle.

But by God, those progeny of Horn Miller's were ornery as all hell. Wouldn't even consider a sale, and as
good as accused himself of having to do with Horn's
demise. It was a trouble this. And especially with that
land right smack in the way of his big spring drive
when he'd push the herd up into the mountains to summer. And now, that wasn't enough he had to trouble
on; there was Sharkey.

The man known as Siringo—and nobody gave a
thought whether or not he'd ever had a first name—sat
in his office in the big log ranch house staring into his
rolltop desk. He didn't know why he had a desk. He
had no need for it. To be sure, he did most of his busi-

ness in his head; for Siringo was not a bookkeeping man. Far from it. The saddle, not the swivel chair, was his element. But he was older now; and he couldn't handle it the way he had in the old days. No one knew that as he did. Nor did he feel happy about the newness of his older years which were seeping in.

He sat there, a tall, lean man, honed by years on the trail, the dust of cows and horses, the smell of men under stress, and gunsmoke and liquor and not enough to eat and the hard ground for resting; when there was time. And there was his purpose. He had built the KT from nothing. And now he was not going to give one inch.

Tall, yes, and stringy, with deep-socketed eyes, a handle-bar mustache, and bony hands with big veins. He sat there in his old swivel chair chewing on an unlighted cigar, as he always did whenever he had what he called "big thoughts," meaning, something on his mind.

Hell, he had figured Sharkey for dead by now. Fifteen years was a good piece of time. And that thorn, that trouble, had been out of his sight this good while. Yet now, here he was back again. Big as always, noisy and laughing. Like he'd never been gone.

And yet, there must be a way to turn the situation to advantage. Because there was still that feeling he had—yes, a sickness it felt like if he ever let it get out of hand—where he did want revenge on that man. And so maybe now he really could get even with the one man who in his whole life had bested him.

Only why, why had Sharkey come to Sunshine

Basin? But Siringo was pretty sure he knew the answer to that. Yes, he reflected, chewing the end of his cigar; it must be for that.

He let his gaze wander to the open window now. It was just getting to be dawn and he could smell the fresh cut of hay that had been rained on slightly during the night; and would have to be turned so it wouldn't burn.

A step on the porch and a knock. The boys back from town?

"Come," he said.

It was Hendry Swann who walked in.

Siringo had swung around in his chair to face his foreman, a man with long jaws and a squint in one eye.

"You delivered?" Siringo spoke around the cigar while he reached to his trouser pocket for a match.

"The boys did. Like you said, I kept out of it." Hendry was a leathery-looking man in his early forties, a good foreman who drove the men hard. The kind Siringo found useful. Useful was the measuring word on any man so far as he was concerned.

The foreman waited a beat, and then when it was clear his employer wasn't going to say anything further, he went on. "Willie got his leg broke. Sharkey throwed him out the window. Had to take him to Doc Greene. He'll mend." He was wagging his head as he told it.

"He still in town?"

"At Sampson's. I lowered him from the window above Sharkey's room, figuring we'd hit him from both sides."

What did you expect, you damn fool, Siringo was thinking. You figure a man like Sharkey is some dumb kid? But he said nothing.

"I reckon Sharkey he is hurting good," Hendry said, hoping for some response from his boss.

"The boys give him a good going over?"

"Sure did. But I mean this." And Hendry placed the blue Deane & Adams on the desk in front of his employer. "No ammo. He must be hurting that way is what I mean."

Siringo looked at the weapon. Sharkey without a gun; like a coyote without teeth.

"Anyhow," Hendry said, feeling a bit miffed by his employer's silence, and lack of praise for a job well done, "he got your message."

"Thing is, will he take it?"

"What if he don't?"

"That's a dumb thing to ask," snapped Siringo, standing up. He drew on his cigar, blowing smoke at the man in front of him, apparently without realizing it; or maybe he did. "I have got a thought," he said. He took the cigar out of his mouth and his gray eyes fastened onto his foreman.

Hendry Swann waited.

Siringo continued to stand there, his eyes on Hendry, but his thoughts were still moving on his plan. A kind of smile started on his face, and moved slowly until it became a soft chuckle. He had it now. He chuckled louder, and then Hendry caught it and laughed too.

"Might be we could get us two birds at one time," Siringo said.

"How do you mean that?"

Siringo said, "Be kind of a funny if a certain place burned down. I mean, like sudden, and no one could figure how come."

"Millers'?" The foreman's thick lids moved back into his head as his eyes lighted up.

"I mean—some place," Siringo said softly. "No name on it. Understand? But it might be something people would wonder how come—like the marshal—and then it might make a concern on how they could lay their hands on a certain famous outlaw who was around, but ain't around no longer. He just took off—and how come?" He picked up the Deane & Adams, his smile broadening. "And that old famous outlaw just happened to forget something . . ."

Siringo looked for a long moment at his foreman, with his forehead raised questioningly, and then he slowly winked. Laughter started in Hendry's throat, but it died suddenly when there came a knock at the door.

At a nod from his boss, Hendry called out, "Come."

It was Harelip Anderson who walked in. No one knew why he had this name, for he had no harelip, only he was minus his upper row of teeth.

"He get on his way?" Hendry asked.

Because Harelip Anderson only had his lower teeth he usually drew his lips together whenever he smiled. He did so now. And then he said, "Me an' Otis seen him."

Hendry nodded and Harelip Anderson turned to go. While this exchange had been taking place Siringo had remained silent. He had moved to the window and was standing there looking out at the long stretch that ran all the way down to the butte that edged Goose Creek.

When Hendry turned to see how his boss had taken the news, he saw only Siringo's hard back.

"Rider," Siringo said, not turning from the window. "Down by the butte."

His foreman reached for the binoculars on the desk. Siringo did not take them. "I know who it is."

The two men stood there at the window while the rider approached.

At last Hendry Swann said, "You want I should whistle up some of the boys?"

"No." Siringo walked to the desk, picked up the Deane & Adams and tossed it to his foreman.

He had returned to the window and was still staring out as his foreman closed the door behind him.

He continued to stand there as the rider disappeared from view behind a stand of box elders. He was, Siringo saw, going to follow the road around the side of the ranch. And now, even though that rider was out of sight, Siringo continued to stay at the window while Sharkey rode closer.

7

It had been simple enough to ride out of town as though he were heading south, and then circle back. And now he really felt the lack of a weapon. His buffalo-skinning knife was all he had but that was no long-range implement. Still, there was nothing else to do. You had to play your cards—no matter.

Riding up from Goose Creek, past the big butte and out in full view of the KT he knew he could be picked off easy as swatting a deer fly. But it was the time for boldness and he was counting on Siringo's curiosity.

Now the sun was up and he could feel it on his back, and when he leaned forward, on the back of his neck. He was chewing a generous plug of tobacco and this caused him to spit a goodly bit. He was still stiff from the last few days' riding, but mostly from last night's encounter in his room. And sore too. But he would not show it. He would simply break himself in; no question on that being the only way.

His eye caught a rider off to the left just slipping down a draw, while to his right another was briefly outlined. When he reached the box elders and dropped from sight of the ranch houses he felt more at ease; although he knew he was still attended. It was a strange moment to lose his tension like that; but he had no time to concern himself. He lifted the gait of his horse and now he rode up a shallow draw and came suddenly right onto the KT's bunkhouse.

Sharkey swore. It was unexpected: but of course it was the unexpected a man had to expect.

He began whistling a little ditty to himself as a half dozen men came out of the bunkhouse and stood facing him, their hands close to their weaponed hips.

He had that habit, besides talking to himself, of softly whistling between his teeth, especially when he was in a tight.

Sharkey did not hesitate. He rode right up to those men and drew rein. And he sat in that old stock saddle on Tom Miller's blue roan, whistling gently to himself as he looked down at those six unfriendly faces.

"What you want, Paw?" A tall young man with long hair almost to his shoulders spoke the words.

"I am come to call on Mr. Siringo," Sharkey said, leaning forward, and spitting a streak of dark tobacco juice at a clump of fresh horse manure. "But first I am looking for a sonofabitch with a scar on the side of his face." And he smiled real cold at those stern cowhands.

"Better be careful with that kind of talk around here, old man," the long-haired cowboy said. "We don't cotton to such words, do we, boys."

At this sally laughter studded the group.

Sharkey eased himself in the saddle, "Sorry, young feller. I should've said goddamn sonofabitch." His eyes were like stone as he looked right at that long-haired man. "Where is the little bastard?"

Before the long-haired cowboy could speak a man stepped through the open door of the bunkhouse. "Right here."

The man was short, dark, and strong-looking. He wore a trimmed mustache and there was a scar along his left cheek. He also wore a very cold smile and a tied-down six-gun low on his right hip.

Sharkey leaned forward on the pommel of his saddle, whistling softly to himself. "I reckon you are," he said.

The man in the doorway laughed. "You got something to back that up, old man?" He took a step forward and stood squarely facing the man on the horse. "This ain't the Old West no more, Paw. You climb off that horse and I'll show you what I am meaning."

Sharkey spat. He spat in the direction of that man's feet. Coming pretty close. And he watched the color fill the other's face, and saw his eyes glitter.

Sharkey moved back in his saddle. He lifted his stetson hat and resettled it on his gray head. Whistling almost silently, he swung out of the saddle. He spat again, not in any particular direction this time.

"I see you want yours truly to have the honor of ending the career of the old, Old West's former gunhawk, who couldn't today hit the side of a barn if he was leaning on it."

The whole group snickered at that.

"I don't have no gun, sir," Sharkey said real innocent, as he started to walk toward the other.

"A gunhawk without a gun! Boys, how about that!"

Sharkey was still moving forward. "Stores ain't open this time of day, so I thought I'd ride out to this here friendly place and see if there'd be an extra." He kept right on walking toward the man with the scar as he spoke. "Like, you could let me have yours."

It was the effrontery that did it. For a split second the man by the door was caught in surprise: for all the time Sharkey had been talking he was walking straight toward him. And now he was right there, almost on top of the other man; and before that gunman had a chance to catch himself, Sharkey, without breaking stride, had kicked him just below the right kneecap. The man with the scar let out a cry of pain and almost fell, as he doubled forward. And Sharkey followed up with a chopping fist just back of his ear. Even before the man hit the ground, Sharkey had the six-gun out of its holster and was covering the group.

"I will talk to Mr. Siringo now," he said, and kneeling with the gun still covering, he removed the gun belt and holster.

He straightened up. "Not bad for a old man—huh, boys." And his smile was real wicked.

No one spoke; they were still caught in their great surprise.

"You on the end. Take me to Siringo. And you others, remember I got him in my sights."

Siringo was still standing at the window as Sharkey entered the office. He had seen the action by the bunkhouse. Now the two men faced each other, neither speaking a word.

At length Siringo said, "I could have had you killed a couple dozen times."

"Exceptin' you didn't."

"I can't promise to control that crew, Sharkey. You were rough."

"I was easy on that sonofabitch."

"Sharkey, I mean those boys out there do not like you."

Sharkey stared at Siringo and his eyes popped open. He coughed suddenly. He seemed to be losing breath as his face and neck reddened. He started to move his arm, as though searching for air. At last words struggled out of him. "You are kidding me, Siringo. What makes you think them boys don't like Sharkey. Eh? I mean . . ." And Sharkey's great laugh crashed into the room. Tears started from his eyes and ran down his red cheeks. He roared. He could hardly stand as his right arm flailed the air about him, and he slapped his thigh. Finally, he had to reach to the desk for support, almost falling under his tremendous mirth. At length he did fall into a chair, still shaking, sucking air as though it was his last moment on earth. "They don't like me . . ." His whole body wheezed with the agony of it. "Siringo, you, by God, have not changed one bit, because I never in my whole entire life have seen a man with such a humor as yourself. I swear to it, by God!"

And the great wheels of laughter again rolled up from his belly and crashed out of his throat.

Siringo had been standing there severe as a Sunday preacher, but he could not keep it up. People never could with Sharkey, he remembered. Now laughter caught him at last. He shook a little, his eyes closed as he joined that old outlaw until at last the two of them filled the room with it; and then sinking into his chair Siringo began to gasp weakly, dabbing an enormous knuckle into his eyes, shaking his head.

It was a long silence they fell into, as each guardedly studied the other. Presently, Siringo opened a drawer in his desk and took from it a bottle and two glasses.

"We will have one for the old days," he said, stern; but a part of him was still laughing inside. He poured, and it was not a Siringo that anyone around Sunshine Basin knew. He poured while Sharkey engagingly watched the brown fluid flowing into each tumbler.

They raised and they drank.

Sharkey sighed, then belched softly in admiration of that marvelous fluid. "By George, that ain't no 40-rod white lightnin' you got there. Course you always did like the good life." And he beamed on his host.

"Didn't you?" Siringo could not keep the frown he had tried to put on his face.

Sharkey chortled at that. "Sure did." He sniffed, looking with great favor on the boss of the biggest spread in that part of the country. "It is sure nice to find myself so welcome here at the KT."

"I have done well," Siringo said, ignoring the little thrust of humor. And he opened one hand in a sweeping gesture as though to include not only his office but the house, the ranch, and the acres around it; and maybe even more.

"I hear you handle quite a few head."

"I manage." He looked at Sharkey. "You have not done so well."

Sharkey pursed his lips at that and, cocking his head, regarded his host through one half-closed eye. "I have done what I wanted."

Siringo's brow wrinkled in surprise. "In Laramie?"

"I kept myself," Sharkey said softly. "I am my own man."

"Fifteen years? I don't know. A man can lose touch."

"Or he can gain it. You learn a lot there, Siringo."

Siringo poured. After he had taken a drink he leaned forward. His face was almost mellow as he spoke now. "Tell me, Sharkey, what do you do for women in there? You know what I mean?"

Sharkey took a pull on his drink and offered it for another refill before replying.

"I tell you, you do for women what you do any place. If you got 'em, you do it with 'em. And if you ain't got 'em, you do it without 'em."

And the two of them roared at that sage observation.

Then Sharkey ran the back of his hand across his mouth, and said, "Now I am in the horse wrangling business. Got me a nice contract with the Army."

At this Siringo's brow lifted in surprise. "I don't reckon you'll be making more'n a hundred a head and for saddle-broke stuff to boot. Am I right?"

Sharkey nodded. "I'll clear a few, make myself a stake."

"Exceptin' that ain't as much as you might figure. Prices being like the way they are."

"How do you mean that?"

"I mean—you're talking to the man who controls the horse wrangling in this part of the country."

"That's what I know," Sharkey said. "One of the reasons I be visiting you."

"I am saying maybe I could make it more interesting for you, more worth your while."

"I am listening."

"I mean—if what you want is a stake, then I might allow to see my way clear to providing same for you."

"I am still listening."

"On condition."

Sharkey's face broke into a grin and a chuckle shook him for a moment. "Same old Siringo, by God."

"Not a big sum, you understand," said Siringo. "But sizable. Yes, I'd say—sizable."

"You said—condition." There was a glint in Sharkey's eyes.

"To leave the country."

"Why?"

"You know that one already."

"I am not here to mess with you, Siringo. I did not come back for that."

Siringo had been looking steadily at Sharkey for some moments. And now he said, "You are—different, Clarence."

And Sharkey was instantly struck by the use of his first name.

"You are not the same," Siringo went on. "Oh, physically—yes. Faster than any of these dumb kids they got around nowadays, but I am talking about something else." He nodded at his own words. "You are different."

Sharkey was still as he said, "There is something I have to do. And to do that I have to be like I was. And when that thing is done, then I can be different." He stood up, putting his empty glass on the desk. "Got a price on that offer of yours?"

"Whatever you figure you'll make on the horses—and plus."

Sharkey's eyebrows shot up. "It is you who is different." He walked to the door and turned. "I seen him," he said.

"That's what I know."

"That part of your offer?"

Siringo nodded.

Sharkey let his hand fall from the doorknob. "It is no business of yourn, Siringo," he said. "Stay out of it."

"I am not interfering; but I am saying that the damn fool don't realize it's only that that's kept him alive."

Sharkey was whistling gently between his teeth now. "No," he said. "He is still alive because he is quicker, tougher, and smarter than you." His big face suddenly broke into a smile, but there was no humor in it. "You are still too soft, Elihu. In the wrong way. That's how you lost her, you dumbbell." He watched Siringo's face darken. "Now you think you can even it by getting me out of it."

Before Siringo could reply, Sharkey's smile brightened and he said, "I just thought over your offer."

"And . . ."

"The answer is no. I am staying in Sunshine Basin . . . till I get my business done."

He was still whistling through his teeth as he walked out of Siringo's office.

The owner of the KT was again standing at the window when his foreman and the man whose gun Sharkey had taken walked in; the latter leaning heavily on a makeshift cane.

"We will have to take him," Siringo said with his eyes on the window, his back to the two men.

"Just say the word, Mr. Siringo." Hendry Swann nodded eagerly.

His companion said to Siringo's back, "He caught me off guard."

Siringo turned to face him. There was a cruel grin at his lips as his eyes took in the man's swollen ear, his sagging body. "Mr. Sharkey always catches you off guard," he said. "Try to remember that if you ever run into him again." He took a fresh cigar out of his pocket. "Yes, he is different." And his eyes were on Hendry Swann.

"Different?" repeated the foreman. "He sure seems like all he was ever cracked up to be." And he wagged his head ruefully.

"He is different," Siringo insisted. And a harsh chuckle fell from his lips. "Fifteen years ago he wouldn't have roughed him up. Fifteen years ago he would have killed him."

8

This day had been one of the hottest, the sun reaching deep into the land, washing down the stems of grass into the roots, heating the brown earth and the rocks and trees. The sun was everywhere, waiting just outside the shade of the town's porch walks, pressing into the frame houses, drawing the smell of fresh horse manure from the dirt street, the odors of flowers from the little gardens here and there.

It was hot in the marshal's office. Tanner sat with his feet on the desk, slouched into himself, trying to nap a little, for he was tired right into his bones. But his thoughts were going too much to allow rest.

His effort to enlist deputies had come again to zero.

Entering the Star or Pastime or any of the other saloons or eateries in town he had made his announcement that he needed men, that while the pay was not great it was not terrible, but that with the cattle coming he needed deputies, men he could count on.

As he progressed through the town, facing the turned heads and averted eyes, the cryptic excuses, the covert glances at his slinged arm, he saw how the stories of Abilene and the other cattle towns had made their mark. And—the fear of Siringo. He was cornered for sure; Siringo had only in fact to wait and he, Tanner, would be quite alone. As indeed he was now. What the cowboys didn't do to the town and the town marshal, the KT hands would. It was a matter of time and the town would belong again to Siringo, who would deal with the drovers on his terms.

In one last hope he had visited the council.

Calhoun and the others had faced him grimly, and somewhat shamefaced. "Clay, we cannot get deputies," Calhoun said. "And, let me tell you, if you weren't here, I don't know who would even be marshal."

"Well, I am here," he said, noting sardonically the different song they were singing from yesterday. They must have really been trying to hire a new marshal, he realized.

Not even the way he had handled Earnshaw, Bowdrie, and Hendricks seemed to instill confidence in them; Sharkey assisting or no.

As O'Donnell pointed out, "Clay, we appreciate the fine way you handled Earnshaw but there are a lot of people figure if it hadn't been for old man Sharkey butting in, Earnshaw would have killed you."

"Well, then . . ."

He had just started to turn away when Butterfield said, "We feel you should let those men go. Turn 'em loose. If you don't, Siringo will break them out of jail."

"That's what I know," Tanner said. He walked to the door of the mayor's office. "That is just exactly what I am figuring on."

"Clay, listen . . ."

Tanner faced them squarely now. "I want a raise. I want more money."

It made him feel good to see the shock run through them.

"How much?" Calhoun asked, his eyes carefully on Tanner.

"Half again what I'm getting now."

He did not wait for an answer. It was not his way to haggle, and so with a curt nod he left.

Yes—everywhere. The only one who offered was Hard Handle Hayes, the town drunk. But, by God, he thought, he would at least take a try at getting some more money. He could leave it for Annie and Tom if it came to that.

There is nothing I can do about it, he told himself, looking at the gun cabinet in his office. There is not a damn thing I can do.

He continued to sit there, while outside the daylight faded and it grew dark; and people began to talk about the chances of rain. But toward midnight the sky cleared, and when Tanner suddenly awakened in his

chair at his desk, he realized he had slept a good piece
of the night. He rose, stretched, lit the lamp, and put
on coffee. After checking his three prisoners, he
thought he would ride out to see the Millers and be
back about dawn. He had a sudden strong urge to look
in on them.

9

The boy Tom was not a light sleeper, but this night, long before dawn began to touch the sky behind the high mountains, he all at once found himself fully awake; sitting upright in his bunk, listening. But there was nothing. Where was Tip? The shepherd dog always slept right outside the cabin, and if there was something not right he would be moving about or barking. Suddenly the thought flashed into him that he had indeed heard Tip barking. Or—had he dreamed it?

"Tom . . ." It was his sister standing in the doorway. "Where is Tip?"

"I thought I heard him barking, but now I ain't sure but maybe I dreamed it." He swung his feet to the ground and stood up. Then he stopped, watching her as she held the lamp away from her as though looking for something in the room.

"Tip always stays outside; what are you looking for?"

"Do you smell something?"

And then they both caught the reflected light on the window.

It was the barn and horse corral, and mostly the shed right next to them that was now crackling high with flames. Smoke was lifting from the log barn, but it was not burning hard. Then they heard the horse scream.

"It's Buck," Tom cried. "He can't get out of the corral."

They could see the bay work horse running in circles, and stopping and turning, his eyes rolling in terror as the fire swept closer to him.

Before his sister could stop him, the boy had run to the corral gate to open it, but the heat from the burning shed was too great and he had to retreat. His hair and eyebrows were scorched; he fought for breath, his lungs pumping against the smoke and heat.

"Throw that bucket of water on me!" he gasped. "I can get the gate this time."

"Don't go there!"

"I can make it. Do it, throw the water on me." But he didn't wait for her. He picked up the bucket and poured its contents over his own head and shoulders; and was running to the corral before she could stop him.

This time he got close enough to open the gate and

Buck came racing through, as the boy staggered back, coughing, his eyes burning, his clothes at the point of catching fire; the girl pulled him toward the house, where he fell to the ground.

"Tom, lie still." Not knowing what else to do she covered him with her shawl.

"I am all right," he said when at last he could get his breath. Then: "All our gear is in the shed; or—was," as he looked hopelessly at the shed which, save for one wall, was now consumed.

"Thank God there is no wind," said Annie. "I think the house is safe."

He was on his feet again and before she could restrain him he had grabbed a pole and was trying to push the burning wall of the shed away from the barn.

Then, even though she saw the uselessness of it, she took another bucket of water and threw it against the side of the barn.

At last the flames seemed to have spent themselves and the fire began to die. The wall of the barn had not caught, but the logs were charred and smoking. The night air was dense with the smell of burning timbers. The shed had completely burned to the ground, and with it, their saddles and harness and other gear, as well as all their tools.

The stars were dimmer now, though Annie and Tom were unaware of the night sky as they began to search for Tip. But he was not to be found.

"He would not have been in the shed." Annie spoke from the horror that was in both their minds. "I mean we would have heard him."

"'Less they killed him first," Tom said, speaking very low. And she heard the tremor in his voice.

Yet the hot remains of the shed revealed nothing that could have borne out the grim possibility. Meanwhile, they had caught Buck and gentled him, and though still spooked, he allowed himself to be picketed in the meadow. The smell of burning timber still filled the night and his eyes were bloodshot as they rolled in fear, while his ears twitched, and he shivered.

They had just started into the house when the bay let out a loud whinny; and this was echoed by another horse from the stand of spruce at the far edge of the meadow. Tom grabbed the Winchester that stood just inside the cabin door and was pointing it at Clay Tanner as he rode up.

It was then the tears started to Annie's eyes, and the boy started to cry openly. When Tanner stepped down from his saddle, Annie came to him and he put his arm around her shoulders.

"Come on," he said after a moment, and he began walking her back to the house. "We'll have some coffee, maybe eat something."

"I am not hungry. Maybe Tom . . ." She didn't finish.

"No," the boy said.

"Even so. It will be good," Tanner insisted gently. "At least some coffee." With his other hand he reached out and touched the boy, who was walking beside them. "Come," he said. "I cannot stay for very long."

As they reached the house he drew his arm away and

took off his hat. They sat at the table over coffee and biscuits while they told him of the fire.

Tanner didn't want to say it, but he did. "I found Tip."

And he waited a moment, before continuing. "He is in that clump of spruce other side of the meadow."

Tom started to his feet, but Tanner held his arm.

"Wait."

"I will get them," the boy said. "I will get that Siringo if it's the last thing I ever do." And tears ran down his cheeks.

"Set down," Tanner said gently. "Do not be so allfired sure it was Siringo." And he drew the Deane & Adams out and placed it on the table.

A long moment passed while they stared at the weapon.

Tom was the first to speak. "I remember it when Sharkey was here," he said.

"Here?" Tanner really let go his surprise. "Sharkey was here?"

They told him of Sharkey's visit; how Tom had shot his horse.

Annie said, "I do not believe he did that. He would not do a thing like that. We talked with him. He stayed here a good while."

"You know who he is, do you?" Tanner said sourly.

"He wouldn't of," Tom said. "It was Siringo." And he said it with finality.

But Tanner persisted. "I am asking; do you know who Sharkey really is?"

"Some outlaw a long time ago, wasn't he?" Annie

said. "We have heard of him. He told us who he was, some things about himself."

"I'll bet he did," said Tanner. "Well, he was the toughest in this whole part of the country, and more than likely the meanest. He faced down Siringo himself one time, whipped him . . ." He stopped suddenly at hearing his own words. He had forgotten that he had known of that episode, until just now when, as it were, the words came out by themselves. But it was the tone of his own voice that had struck him; almost as though he was a boy again telling a story to be praised.

Annie was staring at him. "What is it? You look strange."

"I just remembered something," Tanner said. And he gave a nod as though putting something together. "No —I think maybe it wasn't Sharkey." He stopped, and reached to his shirt pocket for his tobacco. Why had he suddenly remembered his mother telling him not to speak to her of Sharkey?

"It has to be Siringo," Annie said.

Tanner nodded. "Only thing is, how to prove on it."

He built the smoke, lighted it, and got to his feet. "I got to get back; got my prisoners to tend to."

"You still do not have a deputy?" Annie asked, and there was concern in her voice, as her eyes felt over his face.

He shook his head.

"How is the arm?"

"I am all right."

"I will be your deputy," Tom said. And his jaw was set hard as he said it.

Tanner grinned. "Your sister needs you here," he said.

"I want to."

"I will call you when the need comes then," Tanner told him.

Then they went out and found Tip and buried him under a cottonwood where sometimes in the late afternoon sunlight he had liked to doze.

It was dawn as Tanner swung into the saddle. He leaned down for a last word. "I want you to think about you and Tom coming into town; least for the time being."

"We will think on it," she said, and there was almost a smile on her face as she looked up at him.

He knew how it was always useless to argue with her. "Try to get some sleep," he said; and their eyes stayed on each other for a long moment.

The first rays of light were touching the remains of the shed, the charred barn, and horse corral as he rode across the meadow. The acrid smell of the fire was still in his nostrils, and his eyes were smarting. There was nothing in him that wanted to go; only the thought of his prisoners and Siringo waiting for just the moment to ride into town to break them out.

10

It was a time when not a few men worked either side of the law. Sometimes it was the lawman who took the owl hoot trail; sometimes the ex-gunswift wore the badge. The line was thin. And perhaps it was really not so much a question of the law or outlaw, as it was the action. For as the law came with the fences and the sectioning and allotting of land, the free life of the cowboy began to erode, as before him the life of the mountain man and trapper had passed; and of course, the Indian. Fenced in, what could a man do? The body was not made for this; nor the spirit. Sure, there were still the cattle drives and the wild towns, but anyone with an eye could see those days of the free range and the free life were all but gone.

"The cowboy and his life are history," was how Clyde Hollingsworth liked to put it. Right now the doctor was putting it just that way to his patient, the marshal of Sunshine Basin.

"The open range is all but gone. Fences for cattle, and pretty damn directly it will be fences for men." He stood with arms akimbo; his long fingers digging into his back, while he stretched, leaning backward, rocking on his feet. His heavy eyebrows returned to Clay Tanner, who sat on the edge of the examining table, holding his wounded arm on his lap while the doctor prepared for his investigation.

However, Clyde Hollingsworth seldom limited his patients to a mere diagnosis and prognosis on a medical level. His fee invariably included a summation of the situation in the West, the world, occasionally even the universe. At the pouring of a drink—or even without the aid of alcohol—the doctor would discourse upon anything from the quality of horseflesh to the new lady down at Lillian's to the life of the Indian or the price of chewing tobacco. He was chewing now, vigorously, as he did everything, while viewing the "situation"; meaning whatever happened to catch his interest.

"Any fool can see what is happening. First we steal the land from the residents, that is the Sioux, the Kiowa, and etcetera, and now we steal it from each other. We fence the land, and now we are fencing ourselves. The cowboy is doomed. I must say I am not sorry. He is for me no romantic figure but a loud, rude, whining little brat who should be sent to bed spanked, with no supper. When will this country grow up? Probably never. We wallow in our sentimentality and self-indulgence. I daresay Sunshine Basin will indeed be the last of the cow towns. I hope so." He held up a restraining hand, as his jaws continued to work on his tobacco, although Tanner had said nothing. "Don't get me wrong. I cherish freedom. But not license. For most people it is the reverse. Thus, Siringo and the crazy Texas cowboys, and the scum who have drifted into the Basin from God knows where. The thing is, people hate and fear freedom, real freedom. They wouldn't know what to do if they had it. That's why they take it away from everybody."

He bent his eyes penetratingly on his patient.

"Pretty strong medicine, Doc," Tanner said at last when he was able to find a place for the words.

"Strong medicine is not for the weak, Tanner, but it is the only kind that will do any good. Ah—people don't know. They just don't know." He raised his hands high and shrugged slowly.

He went on, his tone still sharp, but speaking now with less agitation. "But I am only a humble observer, mind you. You will see, however, the merit in my remarks. Look on the other hand at that man Sharkey. He is in fact a relic of the past. The good old days!" He snorted. "May they never return!" Suddenly he chuckled, looking at the expression on Tanner's face, which was the look of a man who gazes patiently upon a crazy person.

"I am reading your mind, Tanner. You see, you miss my point. Sharkey is different. He is not mean. Sharkey is alive. I mean—alive! He has got more life in him than half of these galoots nowadays. But what is he to do with it? Eh? Isn't that the question? A man full of life, bursting with it, overflowing, I say! And the country fenced in. The wonderful country gone to hell."

"He has had his time," Tanner said cold.

The doctor's tone changed suddenly. "Why has he come back to the Basin? Do you know?"

"Claims to be wrangling horses for the Army." He shook his head, reflecting. "Course he ain't had much time for it the way things bin. But he does have a contract to deliver saddle-broke mounts; as many as he can get to them before the snow flies."

Hollingsworth was chewing quickly on a fresh plug of tobacco, which he had sliced deftly from a chunk he took out of his pocket. "Fifteen years. God! Do you know what that does to a man, being restricted like that? I mean—a man." He paused. Then, "Ah, yes, he was an outlaw. He killed. But he rode free." He paused again, sniffing. "I see the doubt in your face. But you do not realize that hell is an invention of men."

Hollingsworth snorted. "I have heard that Sharkey and Siringo once tangled horns. Over a woman I do believe." An appreciative chuckle topped his words. "The story is Sharkey bested the Lord of the KT in spades." His face wore a pensive smile. "You know, you and him are a good bit alike."

"About like a tinhorn and a Injun," Tanner said, real sour.

"That's what I'm saying. You both like to handle what's in front of you." He chuckled suddenly. "Well, let us address ourselves to your injury." And for several minutes the loquacious doctor was all business.

The little office above the bank was silent save for the movements of Clyde Hollingsworth as he examined his patient. While the bright sunlight streamed through the unwashed window onto the two men—the one wearing an unbuttoned broadcloth waistcoat with his shirt sleeves rolled to his elbows, the other stripped to the waist, a little white behind his weathered face.

At one point Tanner said, "It felt better getting shot up than getting treated for it."

Hollingsworth turned his head and, taking a step toward the window, spat carefully into a cuspidor. He resumed his examination, his fingers moving quickly, almost as though they knew the job at hand better than he. "The payment is always less pleasant than the tune," he observed. "I thought I told you to rest that arm and yourself. Of course, you didn't. Only natural. No one ever listens to Doc. Except," he added sardonically, "possibly God." Suddenly he straightened. "Goddammit to hell!"

Before Tanner could ask what was the matter, Hollingsworth had crossed the room and picked up a saucer and a pitcher of milk. "Forgot the cat," he said. He sniffed. "Milk hasn't turned yet." Carefully, he poured and placed the saucer on the window sill.

In another few minutes he had completed his examination. "You can get dressed."

For a long moment he studied Tanner while the latter struggled into his shirt. The doctor did not help him. At last he said, "Let me give you a word of advice. It will go unheeded, no question there; yet I am offering it all the same. It is as follows: resign, retire, get out of Sunshine Basin, or at any rate, quit your job. Your arm is useless and it may never recover, but I will have to see. Certainly it will be no good for the next few months or so. After then I will know more."

"That is a helluva big help!"

"Do not get snotty with me; you came to me for help and I am giving same. You continue in that job and you are a dead man. If you cannot see that, you are pretty damn dumb."

"And the law, the town?"

"Let them get someone else."

"There is nobody else."

"You are a fool. A damn fool. You have been a good marshal. The best this undeserving town ever had. But you are through. It is no longer your problem. You cannot stop those cowboys and Siringo. You know it, I know it, everybody knows it. Especially Siringo knows it. Hell, man, can't you see why you cannot get any deputies!"

Tanner stood up. "Doc, that is what I know."

"Then act on it."

"I am doing what I am doing," Tanner said, stubborn. He put his hat on and, nodding to Hollingsworth, walked out of the office.

It was already that time of day when a man could close his eyes and smell the evening that was coming. The sun had passed behind the mountains and now there was a sudden chill in the air. There were no clouds, only a deeper shade of blue in the enormous sky.

Tanner had almost reached his office when he saw the two riders as they came from the far end of town. The Texas yell cut into the street like a knife slicing right to the bone, while they bore down at the gallop in a giant cloud of dust.

He felt the knot tighten in the pit of his stomach and he let his breath go out as he raised the shotgun and walked into the middle of the street.

The Greener was pointed right at the two horse-backers as they drew rein in front of him.

They were young, bearded, covered with trail dust, and their mounts were lathered. But there was no stopping them; their eyes were wild and laughter was roaring out of them.

"My, looky here—a one-armed marshal, by God!"

"And with a popgun to boot!"

Tanner felt the street suddenly go quiet and empty around him. "There is no racing horses in this here town," he said. "Case you didn't or couldn't read the sign down where you come off the trail. And no guns. You can check them at the Silver Dollar." His words were as smooth and even as a milled board. Then he added, soft, "Other than that, boys, you are welcome in Sunshine Basin." And after a beat, "This time."

The dark-haired one started a grin, turning to his lighter companion to say something. But he stopped. The click of the shotgun hammer drawn back was as loud as a rifle shot in the deserted street.

"I mean right now," Tanner said.

"Sure enough, Marshal," the dark one said, real sober. "Sure enough. Where is this here Silver Dollar place?"

Tanner pointed the shotgun. "Thataway."

His eyes were still hard on them as they turned their mounts. "And you walk them horses."

"Yessir."

They had gone only a few feet when Earnshaw's high voice cut out of the window of the jail, which was connected to the marshal's office. "You boys gonna ride back to the KT and tell Siringo you got faced down by a one-armed has-been! What kind of yeller bellies are ya!"

Tanner had turned his head just slightly so that the riders were not quite fully under his scrutiny, but it was enough. The dark one was swift as a striking snake. The bullet clipped Tanner's hat but did not dislodge it. He had raised the shotgun and dropped to one knee. But before he could fire, another shot, almost obliterating the first one, cut into the scene and he saw the dark man clutch his shoulder and start to sag in his saddle, while his companion tried to grab him.

As Sharkey's voice barked into the street, "You boys take it cool, or you'll be buying permanent residence in this here town."

And now Tanner saw him, Sharkey, as he stepped out of the marshal's office, gun in hand, a broad smile on his face.

"Git!" Tanner pointed the shotgun at the two riders. "Next time I won't let you ride out." He spat. "Get on back to Siringo and tell him."

As he walked toward his office with Sharkey beside him he said, acid as a lemon, "So what were you doing in my office?"

"Waitin'."

"Waitin' for what?"

"For to see you, Marshal," Sharkey said, all agreeable.

"See me for what?"

"To see if you'd like to hire me on as deputy. I always bin pretty handy with a gun." And the smile spread all over Sharkey's face.

11

Tanner did not waste time. Opening the desk drawer he took out the Deane & Adams.

Sharkey started to hum a little tune.

"Yourn, ain't it."

"Last time I seen that weapon was when I cracked one of Siringo's jackasses with it and the sonofabitch fell out of my window."

"You telling that straight?"

"I ain't used to having my word doubted, Marshal."

"You are talking to the law now," Tanner said.

"Son, you sure do put me in mind of the warden down at Laramie. He was all piss and vinegar, too, but he learned to trust old Sharkey."

"I have not got time to fool around. You tell me the straight of things."

Sharkey sighed.

"Marshal, I will tell you the straight of it, and it is like this." And then Sharkey told how it had happened in the New York House when the three Siringo toughs had beaten him and taken his gun. "Course, they was three," he added in explanation.

"And then what?" Tanner asked him. "What happened after that? And where did you get that handgun?" He nodded toward Sharkey's belt. "Hell, you know you ain't supposed to be wearing that in town!"

"Took it off of a feller out at Siringo's KT," Sharkey said, looking a little sheepish.

"Jesus," Tanner said.

Sharkey nodded toward the street. "Hell, I thought them two you braced was Fahnstock men, or I'd of for sure put holes in the both of them." He wagged his big head reflectively as he spoke, and pursed his lips then. "I heard about the fire out to Millers', so I can guess where you found my gun." He sniffed again and rubbed his lumpy nose with the back of his wrist. "Figured to pin it on old Sharkey, they did. But, boy, you are too smart a lawman for that jackanapes' plan." He sniffed. "It's how come I am volunteering to be your deputy." And his smile was bright. "Anyways, that's a real pretty little lady out there. Now why don't you get yourself hitched up with her, Marshal?"

"Siringo is a helluva lot more than just some jackanapes," Tanner said, feeling his face color. "And I am telling you I do not want you and him tangling here in

Sunshine Basin. I aim to keep the peace, like I have already told you."

"Son, you cannot keep any peace long as Siringo is about. I know him from old times. Only one way to stop Siringo."

"It will be the law," Tanner said, hard. "And I am telling you that flat out."

"The only law Siringo understands is the same kind as them two just rode in—Colonel Colt's law." And Sharkey nodded his big head and lowered one eyelid in emphasis.

Tanner stood there looking at him, wondering what could you do with someone like that.

"The hell you say," he muttered, half to himself. Then he opened the desk drawer again and this time took out a tin star. Holding it by one of its points, he looked steadily at Sharkey.

"You will take orders from me and not from nobody else. That goes for the mayor or any of the town council."

Sharkey nodded, solemn as he accepted the star and pinned it on his shirt.

"I will be needin' some shootin' equipment," he said.

"'Pears you helped yourself already," Tanner said, looking at the broken lock on the gun rack.

Sharkey looked sheepish again as he said, "I am sorry about that, Marshal, but when I seen you had your hands full with them boys, I was fearing I might run short. It happened to me once before; when I got taken at Medicine Bow."

Tanner said, "I ought to lock you up, if I had any sense."

Sharkey said nothing. He just stood there humming softly to himself.

In a moment he said, "Them Texas drovers now, Fahnstock's boys, they'll not be ornery-mean like Siringo's bunch. Only full of mischief. They're kids."

"Mebbe," allowed Tanner. "But a .44 is a .44 no matter what age the finger on that trigger."

Sharkey had been cutting a strip from his plug of tobacco. He stopped and looked at Tanner now, his whole face lighting up. His voice was filled with admiration as he said, "Marshal, by God, that is true." And he nodded appreciatively as he returned to his tobacco.

Tanner cut his eye at him fast then, checking for sincerity or humbug; but he really wasn't sure; that old man was all kinds of things.

"Those Siringo boys are all trouble," he said. "More than any Texans, I will allow. I do not aim for us to be easy on any of them; Texan or KT."

"Marshal, I never was much good at halfway; I mean like it's got to be all or nothing. No point any otherwise." And Sharkey let out a boom of laughter.

"And I am saying you ain't much good at hiding your light neither."

Old Sharkey chuckled at that. "My paw told me one thing and it was like this: 'Son,' he said, 'if you don't blow your own horn, who will?'" His face suddenly contorted as he searched with the nail of his little finger for a stray piece of tobacco in one of his back teeth. Then he resumed. "Course, on the other side, my maw was real smart too—like telling my kid brother that any boy who'll play at cards on a Sunday will end up on the gallows time he's twenty-one." He sniffed, looking at the offending piece of tobacco on the end of his finger, and flicking it away. "Maw was sure right. Poor Robert."

"Siringo will be riding in for Earnshaw and them," Tanner said, nodding in the direction of the jail.

"Figures."

Tanner lifted a pair of Colts and a two-holstered belt from the gun cabinet and put them on the desk, nodding to his new deputy.

"Two, eh," Sharkey observed, reaching for them.

"You will need extra, even if you don't use your left."

"I kin shoot perfect with either hand," Sharkey said, chewing more swiftly as he examined the weapons. Then, "Fact, Marshal, one of them eastern newspapers wrote about me one time and they said, 'The outlaw Sharkey is like greased lightnin' with *either* hand.'" He smiled quickly. "I got that piece from the newspaper in my war bag along with some other writings about myself. I'll bring 'em all in for you to look over."

"You don't need to," Tanner said, cool. "I can just listen to you."

To which Sharkey answered straight without a flicker, "You know that might be better at that. Like more real-like."

"Course," Tanner went on, "if we should be worryin' about our prisoners making a break, you can read them papers to them. Make sure they stay good and asleep."

And with a short nod and solemn face he walked out of the office.

Sharkey walked over to the mirror. It was cracked and dirty and the image that came back to him did look lopsided, but it was enough of a likeness. He stood there for a moment or two, sizing it all up. Then he adjusted his hat. He unpinned the star and started to put it higher on his chest, but then rubbed it on his sleeve to see if it would polish. He tried it at two or three different places on his shirt before being satisfied. Then he undid his gun belt and strapped on the two Colts. By God, they did feel good. After all those years. He stepped back now, cocking his head and looking at himself from beneath lowered lids. By God, he thought. And he began to whistle out loud.

The door opened suddenly behind him and he saw Tanner in the mirror.

"You sure look good," the marshal said, friendly as vinegar.

Sharkey just beamed. "That's what I know," he said.

"Fahnstock's boys is here," Tanner said, going to the gun cabinet.

And as he spoke they heard pistol shots, the galloping horses, and the Texas yell.

"We will let them ride through a few times," Tanner said. "Let 'em pick their spot for drinking. Then we will make our play."

He put down the shotgun and began strapping a six-shooter to his left side. It took awhile with one hand, but Sharkey did not offer to help. He watched Tanner loading his pockets with shells.

"I got my right arm shot up oncet," Sharkey said. "Learned to shoot with my left. Best thing ever happened to me."

Tanner picked up the shotgun. "It is time," he said. "You just back my play."

"That is what I am aiming to do," Sharkey said, as he followed Tanner out into the street.

12

This night there was no moon, and as the two men stepped into the street they had quickly to adjust to the dark. Most of the townspeople had retired upon hearing those first pistol shots and hoofbeats. In the houses of the town, curtains were drawn and lights were either extinguished or the wicks lowered. Nobody wished to offer the temptation of a target.

It was common talk how things went in other cow towns when those wild cowboys came off the long drives from Texas. Many had seen Abilene and Newton and other cattle rendezvous at the height of the "season" when it was hardly safe to walk the streets some nights. Nor was the state prohibition law going to help, for Sunshine Basin was simply ignoring it.

The marshal and his new deputy stood in the dark alley beside the office they had just left and watched the street. There were four of those raunchy cowboys come to call; only the vanguard of what would follow. And, as Tanner had figured, those rowdies were soon overruled by thirst, and so after a few passes up and down Main Street they hitched their steaming ponies to the rail outside the Silver Dollar. They had tarried long enough in their riding exercise to obliterate with bullets the sign that instructed all visitors to Sunshine Basin to leave their weapons at the Silver Dollar and to refrain from racing their horses in the street.

Only the first batch of thirsty, horny, fun-loving cowpokes; yet it was upon these, the marshal well knew, that the first impression had to be made. Tanner realized too that an inch given to the cowboys would be a mile taken by Siringo and the KT bunch.

"Take the other side," Tanner told his new deputy as he started along the street. Somehow, he could not account for it, but he felt uneasy; and it was not just the Fahnstock riders. What was it? But he had no time to study it now.

About the only lights visible were those that blazed from the Star, the Buffalo Bar, the Silver Dollar, the Pastime, and some other places of pleasure, liquid and otherwise. Save for these bright islands of excitement Sunshine Basin was silent.

The two lawmen reached the Silver Dollar without incident, joining each other by prearrangement in the alley that ran alongside the building.

They stood there listening to the tinkle of the piano, the laughter, and now and then, a random gunshot.

"You could hear that racket all the way out to the KT, I'll be bound," Sharkey observed.

For some reason, Tanner found himself caught by those words, wondering about his deputy's famous confrontation with Siringo in the past. And he suddenly remembered Hollingsworth's telling him it had been because of a woman.

Only there was no time now for thoughts.

More gunshots rang out inside the saloon, and the laughter grew even louder.

"Figger there be some twenty people in there with them cow waddies," Tanner said.

"Give or take."

"So we for sure cannot worry over somebody catching lead."

"Anybody with sense would be home in bed like any honest citizen," Sharkey announced wryly.

"I will go in the front," Tanner said.

"You want I take the back?"

"Better you wait," Tanner said. "I will draw them to the front, somebody is bound to figure on the back. So you come in the front, follow me when you get the right feel of it."

Sharkey cut his eye quick to Tanner's sling. "You are going in alone."

"That is what I am doing."

Sharkey nodded and began whistling softly between his teeth. Then he reached into his pocket and, taking out a plug of tobacco, bit off a sizable chew.

Tanner waited. He seemed to be listening. Then he stepped out of the alley and onto the boardwalk, and walked through the batwing doors of the Silver Dollar saloon.

The attention of everyone was on a group clustered around the piano. The piano player, a diminutive individual named Chip Minor, was frozen in his chair as one of the Texans stood over him.

"Hell, let's see if you can dance! 'Cause you sure as hell can't play that pianner!" The Texan roared the words and now drew his six-shooter and fired at the piano player's feet.

"Dance! Get off it and dance!" In a jiffy his three companions had joined the frolic and were firing at the little man's feet while he hopped and skipped and just barely kept from falling.

Tanner stood just inside the doorway. Two or three of the clientele had seen him enter and he made a signal for them not to draw attention to his presence. The Texans, for their part, were too engrossed in their shenanigans to realize the law was at hand. Tanner waited until the firing had stopped.

In the sudden silence the muffled sound of three gunshots somewhere out in the street could be heard. Was it Sharkey, Tanner wondered. But the thought slipped past. Sharkey should be directly outside the saloon, he realized.

"Hell, I got to reload," shouted the Texan who had started the action.

"Do not waste your time," Tanner said then, stepping forward, and with that ugly-looking shotgun pointed right at the group of cowboys. "I will take those guns. Just hand them to Mr. Minor there."

The piano player was shaking all over. His face was white, there was sweat pouring down his cheeks.

"Give him a drink," Tanner said to the bartender.

It was definitely what was needed, and Chip managed to pull himself together and collect the Texan artillery.

"Marshal, we were just having a little entertainment," one of the Texans put it.

"You are going to have your entertainment without your guns and without your horses too if you run 'em in the street again."

Tanner moved further into the room, easing toward the back. There was something he did not like. He could feel it in the back of his neck. Of old he had known that sign, but right now he was not able to figure its source. He had them covered with the shotgun. But you never knew in a situation like this. Some crazy who was not even with them might take it into his head to make a play. Tanner did not know why he felt so uneasy, but it was there. Yet, there was no time to do other than what he was doing.

He said, "This is a warning. Next time you will spend time in jail." It was as he said those words that he knew what the gunshots down the street had been.

He had turned to face the side of the room now and it was in the next split second that he heard the click of metal. He dropped and whirled, bringing round the shotgun, moving so quickly he was oblivious to his bad arm. Suddenly he was on his back on the floor simultaneously with the crash of gunfire.

It was at this exact moment that Sharkey stepped into the saloon and shot Charlie Earnshaw right between the eyes and Bowdrie in the throat. Both fell dead to the floor.

"Get the Doc," Sharkey said, cool as a whistle, and he had that whole room covered with his two guns as he stood there with his back to the wall facing the bar. That room was frozen solid. No one present would quickly forget the speed, the accuracy, nor the finality of that shooting.

Sharkey said, "I am Marshal Tanner's deputy. Any argument on it just let me hear it." He pointed the weapons at the cluster of cowboys. "Next time you ride in—and tell it to Fahnstock—no guns. Now git on and git out!"

He watched them file out just as Doc Hollingsworth hurried in. Tanner was unconscious, but alive.

Swift as silk, Sharkey brought those six-guns back to their holsters. "I will take a drink of whiskey now, bartender," he said. "And you better get some men to clean up this here place. There's another one outside 'ceptin' he ain't dead."

Men stepped forward and lifted the two bodies to take them to the undertaker's. As they were carried out, Sharkey nodded to two other men seated at a table. "Don't forget Hendricks outside. Siringo's men busted the jail so you'll have to ground-hitch him to the bars till I get there."

He lifted his glass of whiskey, his blue eyes bright

with pleasure. "Sonofabitch woulda got the marshal in the back if the other two'd missed."

Meanwhile, men had carried Tanner to the bar and laid him on top of it. Doc Hollingsworth went to work.

Drinks were poured, the atmosphere thawed, though it was plenty nervous still in the saloon. Now the customers drank, conversed a little, and waited while the doctor probed.

"Sonsofbitches got the same arm," Hollingsworth said, as Sharkey handed him some refreshment. He downed the whiskey, exhaling loudly in response to it.

"How will it be, Doc?" Sharkey asked.

"He will be all right, but I don't know if we can save that arm." He looked at the star on Sharkey's shirt. "Looks like you inherited yourself a job, mister."

13

He lay in the bed with his arm throbbing and watched Annie moving about the room. It was good watching her. She moved easily, her movements as direct as her glance, her words.

It was his room, which he rented from the Olsens, yet she had made herself at home, finding her way about the house, and with the old couple, with perfect ease.

"What can I get you?" She smiled fondly down at him.

He thought she had the clearest eyes he had ever seen on a human being. "You can get me a new arm," he said.

She gave a little laugh at that. "And what about your old arm? You just want to throw it away after it has served you all these years? That's not very nice."

"You got me there, miss," he said.

She reached down and arranged the bed covers and then waited a moment as though there was something on her mind.

"Clay . . ."

"I know what you are going to say."

"Then why don't you really do it this time? You can't go on like this. Next time . . ." Her eyes clouded and she turned away.

"I will think on it," he said.

She turned to face him again, and sighed. "No you won't. I know you. I just thank God you were hurt—and not killed."

"I was lucky."

"Dr. Hollingsworth told me."

"Can I have some water?"

He wanted to think. Yes, he had certainly been lucky. Lucky to have Sharkey there. And how dumb not to have figured Siringo would spring his boys at that very moment and set up a shooting using the Texans as cover.

It was his lack of foresight that bothered him more than his wounded arm. But one thing was clear as a hatful of spring water; Sharkey had saved his life and Sharkey was now the marshal of Sunshine Basin in fact, if not yet in title.

"Here is a nice cold glass of water," Annie said, coming back into the room. "And you have a visitor."

He raised his eyebrows. "Calhoun?"

"Your new deputy, Mr. Sharkey."

He nodded. "Good enough." And he noted the quality of her smile then. It was clear that Sharkey had won her. Wouldn't you know. He let himself relax into the bed. He could feel the tiredness in every part of his body. Nor was the pain easy. It too seemed to spread out from his arm to inhabit the whole of him. Hollingsworth had given him painkiller, but even so. When Sharkey walked in his arm seemed to be throbbing even more.

"Me an' Doc figure you got one of them magnets in that arm of yours, son. Why you attract all that lead."

"How is the town?"

"Peaceable. Couple Siringo men rode in for Earnshaw and Bowdrie. Reckon they will plant 'em out to the KT." Sharkey took out a wooden match and put it in his mouth to chew on. "I do expect we'll be hit again when they come for Little John in the caboose."

"That is a gut," Tanner allowed, and he began to sip the cold water Annie had brought him.

Sharkey was grinning.

"Calhoun or the council get hold of you?" Tanner asked.

"Him and some heavy-set feller."

"Beard?"

"Like a stack of hay."

"Butterfield," Tanner said. "They put you on the payroll?"

Sharkey nodded, his grin spreading even wider. "Marshal's pay." He straightened up, proud. Then, reaching to a back tooth with his little fingernail, he explored for a moment, without letting the wooden match fall from his lip. Successful in his search, he removed his finger and said, "Told them I couldn't live on less; I mean that piddly deputy pay."

Tanner took that easy, though Sharkey's go-to-hell manner did gravel him.

He said, "It is a good job and a good town." His eyes measured Sharkey as he spoke. "So long as you play it straight."

"You figurin' I won't, huh, Marshal."

"I am just telling it."

"That's what I know," Sharkey said, "you are telling it; but you could try trusting your one and only deputy, seems to me anyways."

A strange smile suddenly touched Sharkey's eyes and mouth. "Why don't you thank me for saving your life, Mr. Tanner? I mean, like it has been two-three times now."

Tanner put down the glass of water he had been holding. There was absolutely nothing unfriendly in Sharkey's words.

"Thanks," Tanner said, cold as the water in the glass.

Sharkey stood up, as though something had been settled. "Good enough," he said, and his smile was easy.

"Exceptin'," Tanner put in abruptly, "might come a day when you'll wish you hadn't."

Sharkey dropped one eyelid in a slow wink while keeping his other eye wide open. "Might."

Tanner raised up on his good elbow, wincing even so at the pain that was suddenly activated. His eyes were cold and steady as he looked at Sharkey. He nodded at the star on the new marshal's shirt. "I am lending it to you for a spell. I expect you to take good care of it."

"Your badge is in good hands, son. By the time you come back to work this here town will be as tame as a Sunday sermon."

"You keep the peace," Tanner said. "But you don't have to kill everybody to do that."

Sharkey was whistling softly between his teeth, and for some moments he did not speak. Finally he said, "I will clean up Sunshine Basin. And that will mean I have to kill Mr. Siringo at the same time."

"It will be you who gets killed, you damned old fool," Tanner said angrily. "Listen, this is not the Old Days. This is now. All that guts and guns malarkey is long gone. You got yourself a dead horse and whip with that song, old man." He lay back, disgust all over his face, but feeling better for having spoken his piece, and yes, for giving it to that damn Sharkey, too. "You been lucky up to now," he said. "We both been lucky."

"Fact is, Marshal, there is just no such a thing as luck. The man who is first is not lucky. He is smarter and faster and tougher." Sharkey's words were soft now as he said, "I am only saying that Siringo will have to be handled; and there is only one way he understands."

"By God, you work within the law," Tanner snapped. "I mean what I am saying." And he raised himself up again on his good elbow and looked like he was even planning to get out of bed.

Sharkey held up a restraining palm. "I am law-abiding, Marshal. I want you to know that." A grin started across his face. "Course, it ain't always easy to figure on who is the law and who is not. If you know what I mean."

"Meaning?"

"The law is what the man with the fastest gun, the most money, and the most friends in high places says it is," Sharkey declared. And his eyes opened wide and innocent, while he spread his big hands; his whole attitude one of wonder at the obviousness of such a clear view. "You for sure know that same as me," he went on. "But I will go with the law, like you want it," he added quickly. He rose then and started toward the door. "How would you go for some real painkiller?"

"It took you long enough to ask," Tanner said, his mood breaking.

Sharkey winked, and coming forward he withdrew a bottle of liquor from inside his shirt.

"Good enough." Tanner smiled. "Looks like you might make a half decent lawman at that."

And Sharkey laughed so hard he fell into a coughing fit. When he recovered he took a long drink and then said, "Better cache that bottle, son." And he grinned widely.

After his visitor had left Tanner lay back, trying to sink deep into the bed, hoping for merciful sleep. The drink had warmed him and he found he was able to relax and in fact felt better than he had since Hollingsworth's visit of the day before. He closed his eyes now and let his body go as much as he was able, with his thoughts playing over yesterday's scene with the doc-

tor. It had been then that Hollingsworth had told him
his arm definitely would never fully recover.

"That arm, it just ain't going to ever be what it was,"
was how Doc had put it. "You'll maybe get to use it
some; but only maybe, I am saying. There'll be no gun
action, you can count on that."

"The hell you say."

"That is the way it is, Clay. You're lucky I didn't
have to separate that limb from you." Hollingsworth
shrugged. "What else can I tell you?"

"Damn!"

"I am sorry, Clay. But dammit to hell, I warned
you."

Tanner had sworn again. "All right then," he said.
And Hollingsworth had nodded appreciatively at
that.

He fell asleep now, thinking about his talk with Hollingsworth the day before. But not for long. This time
his visitors were Calhoun, Carew, and Butterfield.

"Better swear in Sharkey as marshal of Sunshine
Basin," he told them.

"You recommend him, do you?" Butterfield looked
his surprise.

Tanner waited a beat. "I recommend him as much as
I would anybody with a fast gun. About his judgment,
I am not so all-fired sure."

"How do you mean that?" Calhoun asked.

"I mean, I don't know him. He is not one you can
get previous with, for sure. But that's the kind that is
needed."

"Like yourself, I would allow," said Carew with a smile. And the others chuckled.

Calhoun looked thoughtful. He pursed his lips, his eyes blinked rapidly. He said, "You figure he might be wanted someplace? I mean, sure he just got out of Laramie; but there could be something . . ." He let it hang.

"I am figuring there is more to his coming back to Sunshine Basin than he lets on."

Under his heavy eyebrows Butterfield cocked an eye. "Siringo?"

"Wouldn't be surprised," Tanner said. "But there's nothing I could prove on it. So let's wait and see. Hell," he went on, "we got to play cards; we cannot just sit here staring the spots off them."

And the three visitors understood the sense of that.

Calhoun said, "Then it's Sharkey." He stood looking down at the man in the bed. "Clay, get better."

After they had gone he took another drink; and he lay there thinking, dozing, and waking again to go over it all some more, while the painkiller Sharkey had brought circulated through him.

Yes—Sharkey. But for himself it was all over. And slipping in and out of sleep he began to remember scenes from long ago, scenes he had all but forgotten.

And he was with Annie that day when they had climbed the big butte at Red Rock. It was a brilliant Sunday morning and they had brought their picnic basket; and the spring sun was freshly warm on their hands and on the backs of their necks and they could feel it coming through their shirts.

There was no cloud in that tremendous sky. They had sat watching the far horizon, and nearby their horses were cropping the short, sweet buffalo grass, and there was the horse smell even above the sage; they had just shed their coats and they smelled real new.

Golly, he had never seen anyone as lovely as Annie. They had sat there together looking at the wonderful country stretching all around them, and at each other. He could hardly bear to take his eyes from her for even half a minute.

How long ago? Pretty damn long. Before he had hit the trail for Texas; before that time at Elbow Creek when old man Kincaid had braced him over the way he'd busted a calf at the Half Moon roundup, and he had been real tough, riding him all that day and the next until finally Clay had hit him one, standing up to him like a man even though he was still pretty much a kid and Kincaid a full-grown, packing hardware to boot. But he had knocked that foreman right on his big fat can. And so Kincaid had taken to wearing a lump on the side of his jaw looked like a turkey egg.

And then one day when he was holding the herd with the big hammerhead sorrel while the branded calves mothered up, Kincaid had rode up and, seeing as how Clay was packing a hogleg, called him. And this was in front of the whole crew, or a lot of them anyways. Kincaid said it simple; that he was about to daylight that smart-aleck kid and right now. Only that bully had not daylighted nobody on account of that young boy had suddenly learned how fast he was with

Colonel Colt's great equalizer; and accurate too. He had shot Kincaid in the chest, and though the foreman hadn't died he'd come right close, and it was a good while finding out how it was going to be.

So he'd quit the country. His mother had insisted; and he'd seen she was right. Until things blew over, even though he'd been called by Kincaid and it was self-defense. And so he'd GTT—Gone to Texas as the owlhooters put it. It had sure cut him having to leave Annie.

It was a whole three years before he came back for his mother's funeral. And too late then for Annie, who had married. "You never wrote," she told him. "I didn't know what to think." He had not written his mother either.

When he'd heard Siringo was hiring hands he'd ridden out to the KT and signed on. By now he'd tamed a bit. To be sure, no one in the Basin or environs knew that during those absent years he had put in time with a lot of the wild boys down along the border. It was no more than many a cowpoke did when times were tough and you could feel the range closing in.

So he'd ridden pretty loose, sown his oats, the wild ones. Now he still had that hell-for-breakfast fire but it had dampened some when he saw how his mother had lived those last years lonesome, and had died lonesome, still without ever having told him much about his father, or his own early times either for the matter of that.

He had remained in Sunshine Basin, cowboying mostly and fiddle-footed, but not taking off for any place in particular, staying with the KT pretty much. Then two things happened that changed everything. Annie's husband caught the pneumonia and up and died. And then the latest of the town marshals went and got himself buried, and Siringo, before he'd broken with the town and the council, had used his influence and Tanner got the job.

Tanner had always been game for anything, so he took it and pinned the star on his shirt. Then when Annie moved back to live with her father and brother, he found himself rekindling a feeling that he soon realized he'd never lost.

He was just remembering it all now when she walked into the room with his supper.

"Getting shot up has its good points," he said.

"Oh?"

"I mean, like I get some real good meals cooked for me," he said. "And nice company."

She stood by the window looking out for a moment. And then she spoke without turning around. "When you can ride again, maybe you'd like to take a picnic out to the butte at Red Rock."

"Like tomorrow."

She turned and made a face at him. "Not tomorrow."

"Tonight then."

"When Dr. Hollingsworth says it's all right for you to ride."

14

The day seemed to break earlier than usual, although it may have seemed so because the night had been so warm. Sharkey didn't care. He had not slept well anyway, and so he was already up and about by the time the sun began to lift over the rimrocks.

"Out early, Marshal," Heavy Owens, the one-eyed livery hostler observed.

"'Pears so." Sharkey squinted at him for extra meaning.

"That foreshoe might loosen some if it's a long ride."

"I will hold my eye on it." Sharkey grinned at Heavy Owens as he took the reins of the blue roan. The hostler was a hefty specimen, but shapeless and not all of a piece. Some said he'd been kicked in the head when he was a boy. The point was that Heavy Owens was a useful observer. Nosy.

Sharkey tied his slicker behind the cantle of the old stock saddle and then handed the hostler money. "Buy yourself a little warming fluid," he said. "Or better, cooling, these days."

Heavy Owens nodded in appreciation and said, "Hear Fahnstock is past Wind Creek."

"I heerd that yesterday," Sharkey said.

Heavy Owens sniffed, then spat at a pile of horse manure. "See a feller over to the O.K. 'long about a hour."

"Uh-huh."

"Name of Halloran."

Sharkey had his left hand full of rein and the roan's mane, getting ready to mount, but he had not yet stepped into the stirrup. "KT man?"

"I wouldn't want to say."

Sharkey reached into his pocket and dropped another coin into the hostler's palm. Then he led the roan out of the livery and into the street. But he still didn't mount. He continued to lead the horse down the street.

The sun was clear of the rimrocks now, a bright disc in pale blue. There was not a cloud anywhere. Going to be another hot bugger, Sharkey said to himself and moved his hat forward on his brow. He was already sweating, while at the same time watching with great care the street ahead and around him.

The O.K. Eatery was at the end of town, right on

Main Street. But he did not approach directly. At the corner by the bank he led the horse over to his office and hitched him loosely, then went inside. The street, he saw as he looked through the window, was still deserted.

He stood just inside the window, checking the roofline across the street. Belching softly, he passed quickly to the back of the office, opened a rear window, and climbed out into the alley. He was carrying a loaded Winchester. Five minutes later he had reached the back of the O.K.

The rear of this dowdy eating establishment gave onto an alley, which suited his purpose just so, for without being seen by anyone inside he could look in on the premises.

A large man sat at the counter. He was hunched over a plate of steak and sourdough bread, leaning on his elbows, with one hand around his mug of coffee, the other gripping a fork. But, Sharkey noted, he wasn't eating. Even though his plate was full, he just sat there looking now and again toward the door that opened onto the street.

Sharkey waited. He was well hidden in the alley. The man at the counter, he realized, was one of the six KT hands he had faced down at Siringo's. Halloran was still staring at the door, then his eyes went toward the kitchen, which was not within Sharkey's line of vision. It was a cute one. Sharkey was whistling softly between his teeth as he eased his way along the wall of the building until he reached the little kitchen window.

Still, he could not see clearly; he could not lean over for a good view without exposing himself to the man he knew must be inside. He waited. Just then the sun moved across the edge of the building opposite and he caught the reflection in the kitchen window of the second man, the man with the shotgun.

Sharkey took a long breath and let it out slowly. Yes, he could do it. He would do it, by God. He stepped in front of the window, raised the Winchester, and fired. Without waiting to see his hit, he raced to the front of the building; just as Halloran burst out of the front door.

"Right now!"

Halloran stopped dead. His hands plunged skyward, his legs shaking so hard he could hardly stand.

"Turn around, you sonofabitch!"

Deftly, Sharkey removed the other man's six-gun.

"Thought you boys learned a lesson from Sharkey out there at the KT. You are sure dumb. Now, we will just go real easy inside that beanery and you will carry your pardner down to mister undertaker. One move—I say, one—and you will join him for sure as Jesus made apples!"

A small crowd of onlookers had gathered and they followed the new marshal, Halloran, and the dead bushwhacker down to Jay Bronowski, the undertaker. Then Sharkey marched his prisoner to the jail.

It was almost an hour after the shooting that he checked the livery stable. He knew what he would find. Nothing. Heavy Owens had wisely fled. Too bad,

Sharkey thought, as he remembered the money he had given the double-crossing informer.

Then he walked back to his office, mounted the roan, and rode out to his original destination of the morning.

15

It would not have been a very long walk; it was just beyond the cemetery, a private place by itself. But like most horsemen he would not walk a dozen steps if he could ride. And in this instance he also did not want his destination known. So he had ridden out of town as though heading for the KT and had then changed direction.

The mid-morning sun was bearing into his back and his thighs as he rode up the small hill and dismounted.

The plot was kept. It was like her; small and clean and neat. She would have liked it, he could tell that. He had stopped along the way and picked some wild flowers and these he placed carefully by the stone which bore her name.

He stood looking down at this small place he had carried inside himself for so very long. It was not as he had imagined it. No, not at all as he had seen it in his mind those long nights in Laramie. It was her, oh yes; it was her quiet; it was her never pushing or insisting; it was her listening and waiting. Yet never resigned. He had never known her to be resigned. And he found a smile had come to his lips as he recalled one time when she had let her anger hit him over something. What? Ah yes, riding with the boys. She had only spoken out about it that one time; but that had been plenty. He felt his smile widen to a grin as the picture filled in more now.

And, too, there was something else now about this special place. He guessed it must be that after all this endless time he was actually here. How strange. How very strange it was. It was something he did not want to lose.

He did not know how long he stood there, feeling the soft breeze on his face and hands, listening to the birds and the jingle of the roan's bit as he cropped at the lush grass nearby. A jay flew to the stone now and sat there watching him; and another.

Now the word "good-by" came to him, but it was only in his thought; he did not speak it. For it was not the word that he felt. And so he did not say it.

He reached to his shirt pocket and the jays flew away. He stood motionless now looking down at the face in the tiny locket which had never left him. Even when the roan nickered and came over and pushed at his arm with his long nose, he still did not move.

At last he put the locket away and put his hat back on, realizing with a sudden surprise that he had taken it off when he had dismounted.

Still he remained, smelling the sage when the wind stirred, feeling the wind in his eyes.

Then he stepped onto the roan and he rode away without looking back. He didn't once look back. He was whistling a little song just on his breath.

16

How long was fifteen years? Oh, he could see changes; feel them. Nothing obvious. People still wore clothes. Still rolled their own, though there was tailor-mades about. There were more dudes, more fence. More law. Matter of that, the girls were prettier. By gosh, for one bad there is always a good. More or less. Like, for every Siringo there was an Annie Miller.

He smiled, reaching for his cup of coffee on the desk. Real jawbreaker stuff it was. But it was hot. And what could a man do without a woman? No, you didn't learn to cook fancy in a place such as Laramie. Yes, coffee was still the same. And the booze.

But there was more law now. That's to put it, more

talk. More papers, more words. For the Injuns had it straight; no writing anything down. A man had to remember his word.

And yet, there were still other changes. Some things he couldn't quite spell out. Or was it himself? Was he getting old?

He wondered casually now, about the marshal. Why the hell didn't he up and marry that cute little Annie Miller? Cautious, he was. Yes, more than likely. Must be in the blood. Musta got it from her, from his maw. Himself, now, had never been cautious—least not that way.

Sharkey studied it, picking between his front teeth with a wooden match. Well, it was sure she had not told Tanner. Why not? Ashamed, was that it? He could not blame her. Still, it did gravel some. So he had rode pretty free, but, by God, he had never done bad to her. But now—who would ever have figured meeting up with the kid like this. And him a lawman to boot!

He sat there wagging his gray head, his forearms on his knees, legs apart as he leaned forward, while his blue eyes stared into the past. Well, he for sure was not going to tell him. She did not want that, and that was real clear.

Only fly in the ointment was Siringo; Siringo, who had wanted Ellie too, but, by God, she'd had the good sense to see through the highbinder. She had turned him down flat. Excepting, Siringo had then come to him on it, on the prod, like it was his fault for Ellie not wanting him. So Siringo had braced him. The damn fool. You didn't get nowhere bracing Sharkey.

Sharkey grinned all over at the scene he was seeing now when Siringo had got hisself knocked flat on his big fat can. And, yes—but for her—would've got his brains blowed out because the damn fool had drawn. Drawn on Sharkey, by God! And kind Sharkey had just winged him. Worse for Siringo, you could put it, for it had been smack-dab in front of a bunch of his hands; and he'd, by God, had to live with that all these years.

Still, Siringo had his points. You could ride the river at least a little bit with a man like that. Trouble was, it had to be his way. Bugger that! That time though when the Shoshone posse had gotten that close and he'd ridden into the KT and Siringo had hid him, and that dappled gray stud—by God what a pony he'd been!—and turned those angry lawmen south and away. A man had to appreciate a thing like that. Yes, their paths had crossed more than once or twice.

That time out at Kettle butte when Dillingham's hands had thrown a running iron onto Siringo beef and Sharkey'd been called on it; no one figuring Dillingham with his long preacher face had an extra brand besides his Box and Slash. And he had got Dillingham and his foreman—that little sonofabitch with that funny name— and three others right in his sights and rode them smack dab into the KT and made them spill it all right to Siringo. Siringo had liked that. He'd got his beeves back and he'd scored on Dillingham; fact, that was the end of Dillingham in that part of the country and Siringo and the KT were that much the better.

The thing about Siringo was he didn't always see everything so personal. And too, like himself, Siringo rated guts high on a man. Both had guts, by golly. Only Sharkey had more; that was the size of it. Thing was, would Siringo keep his mouth shut, or would the sight of himself open his old anger and make him go to Tanner, 'specially if he couldn't get his way in the town? Because he had gotten personal that time way back; he'd been really graveled that time.

Sharkey sighed, leaning back in his chair. Old Sharkey; the words stood in his mind. Old? No—sixty was not old. Sixty was a good time. The best. For the best time was right now, far as he was concerned. Hell, it was the only time you had so it had best be the best. And Sharkey burst out laughing at that.

At the same time, getting toward seventy and all, a man did have to plan on it some.

These meditations brought him to the horse contract in his pocket, and he took it out and unfolded it. A hundred a head. Not bad—for some forty-and-found saddle poke. But not for the likes of Sharkey. His lips tightened as he studied on it. No, he had a better way. And being marshal now was just exactly what was going to help him.

He began to whistle softly as he thought of Tanner lying in bed with his arm all shot up. Good he was out of it. No chance then of locking horns; which himself surely did not want. So it would work. It would work. It had to. Thing was to pick the right time.

"Hey, you going to feed us, Marshal?"

Little John Hendricks' raspy voice cut in on his thoughts. Sharkey had been tilting back on his chair legs, and now he dropped forward. A chuckle rose in his throat as his glance went to the half-opened door that led to the cell which held his two prisoners. And the thought came to him how a couple of weeks ago himself had been a prisoner at Laramie, and now, here he was, the law.

"It'll be coming over directly," he called out, throwing his eye at the clock on the wall.

"Hope it ain't the usual," Little John said through the open door. "I still got me the quickstep from yesterday."

Sharkey pushed back his chair and stood up, stretching. Coming down from the stretch, his eyes watering, he said, "It's the chef's special. Coyote eyeballs fried in bear grease." As he walked through the door into the room with the cell.

The cell was not large, and the anteroom where Sharkey stood was no bigger. The two prisoners, Little John and Halloran, who had not spoken, were both lying on their bunks.

"Couldn't have some gravy for topping?" Little John was in good spirits, but Halloran was glum. He lay morose on his bunk with his arms folded on his chest.

Little John Hendricks sat up, grinning, and looked over at his cell mate. "Cheer up," he said. "You only been in here a day. Look at the marshal. He was in for fifteen years."

Halloran was silent.

Little John sat on the edge of his cot, his elbows on his knees, and began picking his nose. "Say, what's a old owlhooter like yourself sidin' the law for, huh, Sharkey?"

Sharkey grinned at that. He hitched up his trousers, touched briefly the edge of his marshal's badge with his big thumb.

Sharkey was still grinning, but his words were cold as he said, "It'll be 'Marshal' to you, sonny. And don't you never forget it."

Little John Hendricks looked like he'd been slapped. He suddenly remembered Earnshaw and Bowdrie with those holes in them, and his face paled. He looked at Sharkey, trying to figure whether he was being kidded or not. That grin was still on the marshal's face, but there was no fun in it, none that Little John could see. Sharkey's eyes were as hard as marbles.

Suddenly Halloran raised up on his bunk. "You still think it's the Old Days, don't you, when you could just do about what you wanted with a gun and a bunch of buddies. But you have been lucky. You will find it different with them young cow waddies comin' in with Fahnstock. They are going to take this town and not you nor nobody else is going to stop 'em. Things is different now, Mr. Marshal Sharkey!"

Sharkey had been chewing on a match while Halloran delivered his speech. Now he took the match out of his mouth and flicked it to the floor.

"You are correct, sonny. About one thing. One thing is different nowadays. And it is this: in my time punks like you was not allowed out after dark. Now keep your mouth shut or I will feed you them vittles personal." He stood hard as a fence post, glaring at Halloran, who would not meet his eyes.

"If they take this here town," Sharkey went on,

"which they are not about to; then it will be over your dead body for one. And Siringo's for another. Now shut up. I am thinking on something and you are interrupting me."

He stomped back into his office, slamming the door behind him. He had just seated himself again at his desk when Ollie, the swamper at the Silver Dollar, came in with the prisoners' dinner. Sharkey nodded toward the door leading to the cell.

"Man looking for you, Marshal," Ollie said. "He took his horse down to the livery. Should be here directly."

"Tall, thin feller?"

"Short."

"Bald?"

"I'd say he was hairy."

Sharkey nodded, and inside him something moved. "Good enough," he said. And he walked in to unlock the cell door so that his prisoners could eat. Then he checked the trays and Ollie the swamper handed them in.

"Come back in two hours," Sharkey told him.

When he walked back into his office he found he had company.

"Howdy," said the skinny little man with the crumpled, dusty brown stetson hat low on his head.

Sharkey nodded. He took out a fresh wooden match and put it in his mouth to chew on while he spoke. His eyes calmly took in his visitor, who now drew up the backless chair and began to lower himself carefully to it.

"What took you so long?" And Sharkey cut his eye

fast to make sure the door leading to the cell was shut. "Talk low."

"Touch of the piles," the little man said, wincing.

Sharkey nodded appreciatively at the other man's discomfort. "Better get fixed up directly," he said. "We got work ahead of us, and it means horses."

"I'll be all right."

Sharkey leaned back, his eyes working over the other, searching for an evaluation in the light of what he had in mind. He had known Dutch Tommy a long time, but he wanted to be sure that the years had not softened him.

"You stop anywhere?"

"Only the saloon to ask where you could be located. Sure gave me a turn to hear about that." He grinned at the star on Sharkey's shirt. It was a real grin, for there were at least three gaps in his wide mouth where teeth were missing.

Sharkey sniffed. "Dutch, we got to mind ourselves real careful is what I am telling you now. There can't be even one mistake. You mind me?"

Dutch Tommy nodded, and grinned again, his face parting almost in two, and reaching up he scratched deep into his thick head of hair, pushing his hat back to do so. "Who'd ever figure the marshal to be on the prod," he said, and his tone was flecked with admiration.

"It ain't going to be all that easy." Sharkey leaned forward. He had been tilting back on the rear legs of his chair and now he dropped forward. His big forearms lay flat on his knees and he held the wooden match between the fingers of both hands as he studied the other man.

"Is it still Medicine Bow?" Dutch Tommy asked.

"It will be here."

"How come here? I thought . . ."

Sharkey slowly put the match back between his teeth. "I had figured Medicine Bow for old time sake; but here is better. This ain't no time for feelings," he added.

"Right. And like you bein' marshal."

Sharkey nodded.

"You got a plan?"

Sharkey looked up at the ceiling, speaking slowly as though he was reading it right up there on the chipped paint.

"There is two tellers, a man and a girl. And there is the manager. Across the street. Maybe you seen it. About a hundred yards down from here toward the yards."

"And after?"

"Blackberry Canyon. But first you'll have horses at Whistle Creek. I'll tell you the plan on that after a while. First, you get to know the town here."

Dutch Tommy nodded, a fresh smile on the whole of his face.

"You will be my deputy," Sharkey said. "We do not have a lot of time, but I want the town to know you. I want them to get used to seeing you around. You're a lawman and they trust you. You can come and go. If you walk into the bank anytime it's no surprise."

Dutch Tommy nodded quickly.

Sharkey shifted his weight and opened the desk drawer. After rummaging a moment he took out a tin badge and tossed it across the desk to his companion.

"There is twenty-five hundred head of Texas cattle coming in," he said, "any time now." He sniffed, looking directly at Dutch Tommy. In a new voice he said, "Then there is Siringo."

Dutch Tommy's eyes widened. "Siringo!"

Sharkey nodded.

"Siringo is still around?"

"He is the big candy in this here country." Sharkey suddenly scratched deep into his armpit. "He has took over everything excepting this town and he will take that when Fahnstock brings in his herd. The marshal is shot up; how come I got the job."

They sat silent a moment while Dutch Tommy pinned the deputy badge to his shirt. "Always figured I could make it with the law one day."

Sharkey said, "Exceptin' you are not with the law, mister. You are with Sharkey." And he lowered one eyelid, slow.

Dutch Tommy nodded with swift appreciation at the distinction. "Always figured you was a smart one, Sharkey."

"So did I," Sharkey said.

17

At Horseshoe Crossing the Fahnstock herd was restive. They had reached this small tributary of the Powder the day before and Fahnstock had ordered a halt. This to the great irritation of his hands, who, following their long and difficult drive, and moreover, in the time-honored tradition of all trail herders, were only more than eager to roar into town and wash themselves clean in the attractions of Sunshine Basin.

But Calmer Fahnstock, a man not to be argued, had other reasons for holding the herd than just to allow them rest and a little fattening on that good northern feed before driving them to the loading pens. He was concerned about the rumors of the quarantine that had reached him way back at the Red River and, in fact, all the way north. If the quarantine was enforced, his herd would not be allowed into the Basin and he would have to divert to Honeytown or maybe even as far off as Cold Springs. Not a happy prospect because that was money on the hoof. At the same time, and equally important, he was committed to meeting with his old trail boss, who had sent word all the way down to Pine Bluff that it was important, that there was more afoot than those twenty-five hundred head of Texas beeves. From old, Fahnstock knew that when Siringo sent a message it was to be met.

The boss of the FT brand stood now in the early morning light under a lowering sky listening to the bawling of the herd, a tin cup of coffee in one hand and a chunk of sourdough bread in the other.

"Fixin' to storm some," Tod Mallory, his trail boss, observed, clomping up on his high-heeled boots, to stand there, letting his words come to Fahnstock across a saddle rig that was lying on the ground near the chuck wagon.

"Mebbe." Fahnstock had squinted at the low sky more than once. And he had his views, but he was a man of few words; true to the ways of the country for sure. A tall man, with a trail-hardened, leathery face and hands to match, he looked as though that leather went all the way through till it touched bone. He had a long nose, which he had the habit of rubbing with his forefinger, kind of like a horse rubbing its nose along its foreleg. And he had only one good eye. The sight of the other eye had been lost while its owner had been relaxing in a Kansas City sporting house and some frisky customer in the bar downstairs had taken to shooting through the ceiling. He was just high-jinksing; and it was pure chance that one bullet slashed along Calmer Fahnstock's nose and across his eye. He had lost its sight, but not his anger. It took a good while for him to find that miscreant, but he did; the same now residing in Kansas City's bone orchard.

"Riders coming in," Tod Mallory said.

"I heerd 'em."

"Sounds like a pair, maybe three."

"Three," Fahnstock said, and he rubbed the side of his long nose with his thumb, for he was still holding the piece of sourdough. "It will be our company."

He had just emptied his cup and dumped the grounds onto a clump of sage when three horsebackers rounded briskly a small stand of box elders and drew rein.

"You et yet?" Fahnstock canted his head to one side as he spoke in order to get full value from his good eye.

"Could stand a cup of jawbreaker," Siringo said, coming down from his big bay horse.

Without saying anything, the two men who accompanied him moved off with Tod Mallory toward the cook wagon; and Cookie brought coffee and biscuits for Fahnstock and his guest.

"You made time from the Red," Siringo said.

"Would of took longer, but when I got your message we pushed; though," he added, "I didn't want to run weight off the beeves."

"Good enough."

They were squatting now near that saddle rig, and Siringo picked up a branch of sage and began drawing in the space of bare ground in front of him.

Fahnstock, for his part, was noting Siringo, older now, but by no means softer; not much different than when he was pushing cows up from Texas twenty years ago with his dad. Fahnstock was the younger and Siringo had whipsawed the drive for his paw. Fact, it was Siringo who had located that high-jinkser in K.C. for Fahnstock to revenge on him. So the drover owed Siringo one.

"What's with the quarantine?" he asked now.

"Not to worry on it." Siringo dropped the stick he was drawing with and took a cigar out of his shirt pocket. Offering to Fahnstock, who refused, he put the end in his mouth, after biting off a piece and spitting, and then lighted it. "The quarantine is not a problem. They seen the sense in not enforcing."

"Money is money," Fahnstock observed with a tight smile.

"That is so."

"That leaves the marshal. Is he feeling friendly to us poor Texians?"

"Tanner is out of it." The trace of a hard smile touched Siringo's mouth, just at the corners, but it did not reach his eyes. "He got himself shot up." His mouth hardened then. "You mind Sharkey?"

Fahnstock had been rubbing his nose, and now he stopped and canted his head. He gave a long sniff, right through the whole length of both nostrils.

"He is in Sunshine Basin?"

"He is the law in Sunshine Basin."

Fahnstock put out his hand and took a cigar from Siringo. He lit it and said, "He is still—Sharkey?"

"You could give odds and bet your britches on it."

"How the hell . . . last I heard he was in Laramie."

"He served his time."

"How come he's back in this part of the country?"

Siringo spat. His cigar had gone out and he relighted it, shifting his weight a little, realizing that maybe he wasn't so old, but his knees sure were. "He says he's here on contract for the Army to sell 'em broke saddle ponies. But the council hired him on—meanwhile."

"I do not see Sharkey as a horse wrangler."

"Like yourself pushin' a plow," Siringo said wryly.

Fahnstock studied the sky for a minute and then he said, "You figure he's in the Basin on other business."

"I do that."

"Never figured Sharkey for a lawman neither," Fahnstock said.

Siringo spat a heavy load of saliva at a clump of sage. "He has got Tanner's job, mostly on account of there is nobody else wants it. The town council is easy on account of Sharkey can handle a gun. Now—" He spread his hands open in front of him, palms down. "Now, they want a peaceful town, but they want the cattle trade." He paused, and his eyes were straight on Fahnstock. "I want Sunshine Basin."

Fahnstock said nothing to that. He sniffed. He looked at the sky, listening with a part of himself to the cattle, still restive. Then he looked again directly at Siringo.

"That is why you want me to hold 'em here longer."

"I want your men to be climbing the trees when they hit town; and I want the town worryin' on when you're riding in."

"Four of 'em bust in already," Fahnstock said. "Unbeknownst to me. I can't hold 'em much longer."

"That's what I know."

"How long then?"

"Another day will do her."

"I'll do my best."

Siringo shook his head. "Not your best, Fahnstock. I want a full day. That will give me the right time for it." He spat. "With me running the town your men will have no trouble. No trouble at all. Nor will any of the other herds."

"You will handle Sharkey?"

"He has been lucky up to now. Couple of my men were foolish enough to go up against him; figured he was old, had had his day."

Both men cut a smile at that.

Fahnstock reached up to pick at his long chin. "They are smarter now, you're saying."

"They are deader'n hell is what I am saying. The others seen it. The mistake is a lesson. Next time Sharkey will not get away with it."

Fahnstock was squinting again at the sky. "I figure it might come to fair off," he said.

"Easier to hold 'em then."

"Till tomorrow."

"Let it be noon," Siringo said. "Towns are sleepy 'round noontime."

There was a patch of blue in the sky just above the mountains to the west when Siringo and his men rode out.

18

Meanwhile, the town lay somnolent in the heated afternoon. Thunder was in the air, although the sky was clear; yet the gathering could be felt. People looked at the sky, reading for sign, even though there appeared nothing to be seen.

Sharkey's forehead was damp as he checked his prisoners, checked the guns in the cabinet, checked the loads in the weapons at his hips. He debated whether to go for coffee, but before he could reach a decision, the door of the office opened and Dutch Tommy walked in.

"Looked over the bank did you?" Sharkey asked as his deputy took the backless chair.

"Don't appear like too much of a hassle." Dutch Tommy sucked thoughtfully on the space between his teeth. "There was three. Is it usual?"

"That's the size of it," Sharkey said. "O'Donnell—the old man. And the girl, and a feller name of Harvey."

Dutch Tommy nodded.

"What did you tell them?"

"Introduced myself." Dutch Tommy grinned. "Told 'em I was just getting acquainted; said you sent me. Like that."

"Good enough." Sharkey sniffed. "And the layout."

"One room with two windows and the front door. Counter. Back room with a door to the alley."

"Where is the safe?"

"Back of the counter on the left by the stove."

Sharkey nodded, seemingly satisfied that his deputy had passed the interrogation satisfactorily. Then: "What about guns?"

"I figure O'Donnell has something in his desk drawer. But nothing on him. Harvey didn't have nothing that I could see." He grinned again. "Better for him not."

Then Sharkey said, "You didn't spot the two shotguns by the back door."

The new deputy's face dropped. "Only saw a pile of boxes covered with a old buffalo robe; least that's what it looked to be."

"Dumbbell," Sharkey said. "There is two Greeners, and maybe more under that robe." He scowled. Yet he was not wholly displeased. It had taken himself a while to figure that one out. "Thing is we got no time to fedaddle."

"You got a plan?" Tommy asked.

"We got to plan as we go," Sharkey told him, holding his voice low, after first cutting his eye to the door leading to the cell. "On account of we don't know how everyone will be, or where, when those Texas beeves come in."

Dutch Tommy shifted in his chair but said nothing.

"We will have our plan but we got to keep loose; be ready to change it." Sharkey wrinkled his brow, pursed his lips, sniffed. "We'll be here, say, when the drive hits. First though, you get two horses back in the alley. Far back, not near the street at all where they could be seen. And then fresh mounts at Whistle Creek."

"How do we go in? Front and back?"

A grin touched Sharkey's eyes as he looked at his colleague. "There is a lot of money in that safe," he said.

"That's what I figure," said Dutch Tommy.

"But there is more in the safe in the back room," Sharkey said. "The safe you never spotted."

Dutch Tommy's eyebrows shot up. His lips formed for a soft whistle.

Sharkey ignored his reaction. "You go in the front," he said. "Just friendly. Like you want to put in some of your pay. Or, if the drive has already hit, you warn them to close down. Get the customers out. Get the others down on the floor. You know what to do."

"Got'cha."

"I will come in the back." He chuckled suddenly.

"Also to warn them to watch out for them frisky cowboys."

Dutch Tommy's stubbled face separated into a big
grin. "Like there will be two jobs."

"You are right."

"What if someone comes in?"

"You locked the door."

"What do we take it in?"

"Saddlebags. I will bring them. And rope and something to gag them. You'll have to be fast." Sharkey
stopped suddenly; his eyes were cold as he looked at
the other man. "And do not forget this. This is my last
job. This is my stake. And yours too."

"Got'cha." Dutch Tommy suddenly had a thought.
"What about the marshal; I mean Tanner?"

"What about him? He is in bed with a shot-up arm."

"I hear he is not easy to keep down. Suppose he
hears the ruckus and comes looking around."

Sharkey nodded appreciatively at this; it was a good
thought, and he was surprised that it had come from
Dutch Tommy.

"I will handle Tanner," he said. "If he does come,
leave him to me." He waited a beat and then said,
"Leave Tanner to me. You mind me?"

Dutch Tommy heard that extra something in
Sharkey's voice and he nodded swiftly. "I got'cha," he
said.

Then Sharkey said, "Whyn't you go get us some
coffee? Try Frenchie's. That stuff from the O.K. would
kill a bear."

19

It was again Hank McAuliffe who brought news of Fahnstock to Tanner. But this time Tanner wasn't standing in the middle of Main Street with a sawed-off shotgun in his hand. He was flat on his back in bed with fever.

"The word is Fahnstock's holding twenty-five hundred head at Horseshoe Crossing," McAuliffe said.

"Figuring?"

"Figurin' on his boys gettin' real raspy on the town 'fore he turns 'em loose." And McAuliffe, a big man with a big face, pursed his lips on that.

"Sounds like Siringo," Tanner said, closing his eyes to study it better.

McAuliffe was a knotty man who'd had, he didn't know himself how many, bones broken riding broncs. Now he let his eyes roam around the room.

"Still could use a deputy, Hank."

"Sorry, Clay. Even if you was marshal yourself; I mean active like," he added quickly.

Tanner cut his eye quick at him then. "You favor Sharkey, do you?"

McAuliffe was already wagging his big head. "Sharkey . . ." He grinned suddenly. "He is—all right."

"But . . . ?"

"That deputy . . . I dunno."

Tanner did raise up at that, even though his head was hammering. "Deputy?"

"Feller name of Dutch Tommy." McAuliffe looked questioningly at the man in the bed.

"Don't know him." And he let his head sink into the pillow.

"He looks like a hardcase to me," Hank McAuliffe said.

Tanner's brow wrinkled and his face moved in a sort of shrug. "Any camp in a storm is how we could look at it," he said. "A deputy is a gun on your side."

McAuliffe nodded vigorously at that, hoping that Tanner would not ask him again to take on the job.

"You looking for a drink?" Tanner asked suddenly in a different voice.

Hank McAuliffe beamed all over.

Tanner reached beneath his blanket and passed what was left of the bottle Sharkey had brought.

McAuliffe allowed himself a generous swig, sighing

with deep pleasure as his body acknowledged the bracing fluid. "How is it, Clay?"

"Good enough. I figure to be up and about directly."

To this Hank McAuliffe said nothing; and presently
he took his leave.

Later, when Annie entered the room, she found
Tanner sitting in the armchair by the window.

"You should not be up," she told him, though her
tone was only mildly scolding.

He did not answer, yet he acknowledged her words
with a slight movement of his hand. He was looking
out the window at the long field that spread behind the
Olsens' house. A bay mare and her colt were gamboling
there, frisky as spring. Now the mare stopped suddenly
and the colt, unable to stop, fell into her flank and staggered about on spindly legs, nearly falling, but manag-
ing to regain its balance.

"That is the way to be," Tanner said, his eyes still on
the horses. The window was open and through it came
the smell of the horses and the grass.

He took her hand now and held it in both of his as
she stood beside him.

"Why don't you then?" she asked simply.

"Why?" He looked up at her, then back at the
horses, which were cropping the grass, their tails
twitching at flies, the mare now and again kicking at
her own flank or shaking her head. "Because they
won't let you, that's why."

"You only have to walk away," Annie said. And he
heard the stubbornness in her voice.

She went on. "You've done your share. More than your share. Now it's someone else's turn."

"Whose?" He looked up at her again, and again back to the horses in the field. His eyes were on them as they raced out of his line of vision, while he said, "There is no one."

"Sharkey."

"He is temporary. He will not stay."

"But how do you know? Maybe he will."

"No. I know."

There was something in his voice she had never heard before. "How do you mean that, Clay?"

"Sharkey is a drifter. Sunshine Basin is growing. Someday it could be even a city maybe." He searched for his words for a moment. "Thing is, if you take on a job you've got to live it. It is no good just helping out."

"But now," she insisted, "until the trouble with the cattle and Siringo and all is settled, couldn't Sharkey . . ."

He didn't answer. All of a sudden he leaned forward, letting go of her hand, and stood up.

"Clay, please get back into bed."

He could feel the weakness all through him and the throbbing in his arm, and in his head too.

"No."

"Please . . ."

"I want you to get Tom. Have him saddle my dun horse."

For a moment she stood in front of him, looking into his eyes, and he felt something want to soften inside him. But he would not allow it.

"All right then," she said, and she turned and walked out of the room.

It was sure not easy getting dressed, but he did it. He was waiting when Annie returned with her brother. He had sat down again, this time on the edge of the bed. His head was ringing, his arm ached. He felt weak all over. But he himself was not weak. He knew that. He knew it was that one strength that would carry him. No question.

"Clay, will you please not go?"

"There is one thing has to be done," he said. "One last chance. I got to take it."

She looked pale, he thought suddenly; and again he felt the weakness running like water through his own body.

"I will be back shortly."

"Tom will go with you."

"No."

There was no argument on the way he had said that. He saw the tears standing in her eyes, but she would not let them flow.

Tom helped him onto the dun. It was a hassle handling the shotgun, but he managed. With a nod he pointed the horse toward the town. It wasn't far, but it would be a long ride, he knew. It was the only thing to be done. It was the thing he had to do.

20

Sharkey looked up at the clock again. Funny how time passed. In Laramie it had gone so slow; other times he'd seen it go so fast. Still other moments, both ways it seemed. Like now. Well, it was the way it was. No matter. It would all soon be done with. He felt his side now, rubbing the ache there. It had been a pain growing for a day or two. Age? Or maybe that thing he'd had at Laramie? Kidney, the doc had said. Well, it wasn't bad yet. He knew how bad it could get. Thing now was not to let anything come in except the work at hand. Paw had taught him that. Along with a lot else.

Suddenly a picture of his father came to his mind,

his big, beefy hands holding the reins as he sat his favorite horse, the big blaze-faced sorrel. Old Paw; long
gone now. Planted down there near the Territory. And
Robert too. Except poor Robert hadn't lived all that
long. Robert never did have a hand for the kind of life
himself and Paw favored. Still, he had tried. He had
sure had his guts.

And all at once he was back at that afternoon Paw
had ridden into the canyon with those calves. That was
the day he and Robert had mended the corral gate
where Paw's big sorrel had about kicked it to tooth-
picks, him being ornery like he was. And he remembered how Maw had called them from the porch of the
log cabin to come set the pole for her wash, her hands
still red and wet as she took the bundle of soggy
clothes out of the wooden tub.

It had been when they were walking back to the corral that he'd happened to look out past the barn and
spotted down by the big butte that glint of sunlight on
a concho or belt buckle maybe, then horns, and then
he'd known cattle was coming. And there was Paw riding his big sorrel with the cast in the left eye.

Then he and Robert had run to the round horse corral and climbed up for a better look. When he'd seen
how many calves there were and just a few cows and
steers with them, he figured something was different;
especially when there was F. T. Orlibow and Jake Hin-
deman from the other side of Tensleep. And Robert
had said as how he didn't see no brand on any of them
calves.

And Paw was calling them, yelling at them not to set

there like a couple of stuffed hoot owls but get the running iron from the barn and build a fire, and hot!

Then Maw had come out of the house and yelled at
Paw, fighting again with him about owlhooting and
how he had promised he'd never again, but here he
was. Paw'd been drinking and just didn't listen. But she
went on at him, and finally he hit her one. That didn't
stop her; Maw was tough, so he let her be. After a
while she gave up on it and went back into the house.

And so they'd branded those calves; and now all
these years later he remembered how way back then
just as they were branding he had recollected the time
when about two-three months before that Clanton had
ridden over from the North Fork with half a dozen of
his men, all armed, and had by golly ordered Paw to
show him the hide belonging to a beef he had hanging
from a tree back of the barn. And he, young Sharkey
then, had wondered why Paw at the time the critter
was butchered had right away made the hide into a
rope and before he did that had cut out the brand and
dropped it into the fire.

Clanton saw a hide with Paw's brand on it all right,
one that had been off a steer killed about two weeks
back. He didn't know it had been taken off a cancered
steer, and that Paw had taken the trouble to stick him
and bleed him before he took the hide off so it wouldn't
look too dark. The old man, Paw, sure knew more
tricks than a dozen Clantons could figure.

Maw always claimed he could of been a rich man if
he had only shook a straight rope. But Paw, like himself he'd allow, minded the excitement. Course he'd

ended up gutshot down by the Territory. And Robert—he'd been hanged by a angry posse.

Only himself left. And with him it'd been close more than a time or two. That fifteen years at Laramie was no fun.

Suddenly Sharkey found that he was smiling to himself, remembering a story Paw had liked to tell every now and again, and they—himself and Robert—had not tired of hearing. It concerned a young waddie named Zip Stooder. He was fairly known in the country and then one day he suddenly disappeared and nobody heard anything about him for maybe five years or so. Then he showed up and old John Wainwright, who ran the General Store in Tensleep, gave him a job. And Sharkey, remembering it, could almost as good as hear Paw telling it, and chuckling, and taking his time on it.

Old man Wainwright had told his sons and a friend or two of theirs about it one day, saying Zip was a good fellow to hire, on account of he was real careful and it was a good sign.

"Careful?" his son Freddie had asked. "How do you figure that?"

"Why," said John Wainwright, "I'll be damned if he ain't got the very same suit of clothes on he had when he used to come in the store five years ago."

And they had all busted up over that, for though the old man never tumbled, everyone else knew Zip had been in the pen for those five years.

Sharkey sighed and ran his forefinger across his front teeth. Thoughts. He had forgotten all of that this good while. Funny how it had come back. And now he almost began to dwell on more of it, but he forced himself away. Thoughts, he told himself, is what makes a man soft, what makes him get dead ahead of time.

But in spite of that he found himself thinking of Tanner. Well, it would be too bad. But he, Sharkey, had to do what he had to do. No sense in being the most honest corpse in the graveyard; better the richest. Or in the poorhouse either. He would have his stake, and he would live his next years nice. Move out of the country, toward Hightown, and maybe get himself a spread with a few head of cattle. He could handle that. Nothing big, but something for himself. Like he had long ago promised her and had never kept it.

So the kid would feel he'd been crossed; and right. But that was the size of it. Paw would have sure done the same.

He sat straight up in the chair suddenly, for there was something, some thought somewhere in him, a feeling of something or other. Was it that damn kidney or whatever?

He stood up, dropped his hands to his weapons at his hips. No more thoughts. He had to be like he had been now, like in the old days; no thoughts, nothing to worry on. Just the action. Later, he could be whatever, but now until the job was done he had to be one thing only, like he'd used to be before.

To help himself he crossed to the gun cabinet and again checked the loads.

21

The mayor's office was on the second floor of the New York House. It was a well-appointed room. Buffalo robes covered a part of the floor, and Indian artifacts were in evidence. Carl Calhoun appreciated much of the Indian culture. He could not really have explained why; and while he was not a collector ruled by the acquisitive sense, he favored articles that pleased the eye—colors and shapes principally. Calhoun was not overtly a religious man but he had a feel for the life of the Indian of the Plains. He was rather an anomaly in this respect; perhaps it was something born in him, or possibly he had picked it up while at college back East. At the same time, he was primarily a

politician and as such took pains to see that his interest
did not appear obtrusive. Like all members of his profession Carl Calhoun understood the need to appear
wholly acceptable to his fellows.

Present in the room with the mayor were Doc Hollingsworth, Coy O'Donnell, Butterfield, and Carew. It
was their custom to meet every Tuesday to discuss
town business and policy. This being that day of the
week, they were in session. Indeed, it was just eight
days since Clay Tanner had faced down Earnshaw,
Bowdrie, and Little John Hendricks in the Star saloon
and Sharkey had appeared in Sunshine Basin. It was
also the council's habit, and even their necessity, to
partake of a solid lunch. Calhoun was a man who sa-
vored the material aspects of life and he saw to it that
his table was catered with the best he could afford. He
had found, as many of the rich have before and since,
that the better he treated himself, the better he was apt
to feel toward his fellow man.

Right now, the members of the council were address-
ing themselves to liquid refreshment. They were con-
genial, yet at the same time businesslike.

"So we have inherited the sins and troubles of Ellsworth and Wichita," Hollingsworth was saying.

Calhoun's chubby face folded into a smile. "You expect too much of mankind, Clyde," he said, and
blinked his eyes rapidly.

"On the contrary, I expect no more than the worst,"
the doctor responded sardonically. "We have all seen
what happened to those towns, and others, when they
became cattle terminals. It ruined them, it ruined the

country, it ruined the citizens." He paused, accepting one of Carew's cigars. "But it is possibly our fate," he went on, after swiftly lighting and drawing on it, to release a billow of smoke. "All those fun-loving cowboys. The backbone of the West we are told. Nobody has indicated what part of the backbone, however."

Coy O'Donnell chuckled at that, scratching his bald head. Then, looking at his fingernails: "But we are in the position of having to decide a few things," he said softly. "We have the power to withhold." And he beamed, raising his head.

"Such as?" asked Butterfield.

"Such as the quarantine and prohibition."

"And the new marshal?"

"Him too."

"I am not so sure."

Calhoun placed his hands on the table next to his glass, and everyone knew he was going to come out with something. You always knew where you stood with the mayor, which was why he was liked, and even trusted.

"So we decided against the quarantine and we've got the cattle drive, which is, of course, what the farmers don't want. But what about them; how will we handle the farmers, men like Killigan and Hart? It is not going to sit well."

"We have gone over this a dozen times already," Carew observed. But nobody listened.

"You know how I feel," said Butterfield. "I am in the middle. If I make money with the ranchers, then I lose with the Texans. It's like with all of us." And he looked around the table.

"You know where we stand, Carl," Coy O'Donnell said. He reached for the whiskey bottle. O'Donnell looked a good bit like an actor. At any rate, he took extreme care with his appearance, and was always dressed in the finest. As the town's banker he could well afford it.

Carew opened his long hands, wrinkling his hard forehead. "Where were we before, where are we now? Still in the last depression, while the rest of the country is booming."

"But the price, gentlemen, the price." It was Hollingsworth, his words grainy from his having just finished coughing. "The price is murder, theft, hoodlums, unbridled whoring, and unlimited gambling. And . . ." He held high his right forefinger. "And there is Mr. Siringo."

The mention of the KT overlord brought the company to a new level of seriousness.

Calhoun was nodding gravely. "Yes, that is the question. Now we have opened the box; how do we handle Siringo?"

The mayor carefully spaced his words, punctuating them with glances at each of his companions in turn.

"We are fortunate then to have a new marshal," observed Hollingsworth wryly. "I am convinced of his ability. And moreover, he is swift as a snake with either hand."

"But what is he like, eh? That's the question," Carew said. "Tanner was an honest man. Still is," he added quickly with a short laugh, catching himself up. "All we know about Sharkey is his past; and pretty damn unsavory that past was."

"He was tough enough to go up against Siringo and his men." It was Calhoun saying those words. "And you know, if we don't handle Siringo and pretty damn fast, the farmers will."

"It will be a war, then," observed Hollingsworth, and his tone was biting. He smiled. "A war. Just like Lincoln County. We would lose the cattle trade as well as the ranchers." He coughed out a laugh. "We could even lose our collective bee-hinds."

"It is clear," Calhoun said, "that it hinges on our maintaining law and order. What we have said a few dozen times already," he concluded sourly. And he reached for the bottle and poured liberally.

Hollingsworth downed his at a draught and, relaxing back into his chair as the warm fluid cruised through his lengthy frame, he emitted a great sigh. "Ah, there will be lots of business, I am certain—for our undertaker. And when we have killed off each other, who will be left? I wonder. Will there be anybody left to be king of the castle?"

"Clyde, I have always felt you should have been a man of the cloth rather than the scalpel," O'Donnell said. He took out a cigar and bit off the end. Carefully he lighted it, turning it to take the flame of the wooden match evenly. He released then a rich plume of smoke and, leaning back, rubbed his round belly with pleasure. "Nothing like a good cigar." He chuckled. "As the old saying has it: a woman after all is only a woman, but a good cigar is a smoke."

All smiled tolerantly at that aged remark.

"And Tanner?" Hollingsworth said abruptly. "I vote we give him a good pension."

"He has earned it," said Calhoun.

"But let's not go hog wild," cautioned O'Donnell. "All very well to take care of our ex-marshal, but within limits. Within limits," he repeated.

"Speaking of women," said Carew with a smile.

"Which we weren't," put in Coy O'Donnell. And all chuckled at the overture.

"Speaking of the ladies," Carew persisted. "I am happy to see that the O'Grady is up and about."

"Lollie O'Grady is a delight to the eye, both eyes," allowed Hollingsworth. "And I may add, one of my favorite patients. Fortunately, it was only a dietary disturbance."

"Then she will be back in—er—business, may we presume?"

"Indeed, she not only will be, but is," smiled Hollingsworth. "Our friend, Marshal Sharkey, I have been given to understand, has already sampled the good lady's pleasures, more than a time or two." He chuckled as he watched his companions shift in their chairs while their thoughts hurried to conclude their business.

But their pleasure was interrupted by the door opening.

It was Clay Tanner who walked into the room: pale, drawn, clearly weak on his feet, but also clearly determined.

There was a moment of surprised silence and then Clyde Hollingsworth swore. "Dammit to hell, Tanner, I told you to stick to bed. Don't you have no sense at all, goddammit!"

Tanner ignored the outburst. "Gentlemen, you have got to enforce the quarantine." Ignoring the chair that Butterfield offered him, he stood there, his face hard as a gun barrel.

"Clay, it's too late now to bring it up. We have long ago decided on that," Coy O'Donnell reasoned. "Fahnstock is at Horseshoe Crossing."

"I know where he is. He can still be told. He can swing over to Honeytown."

"But he won't. He'll lose money. And Siringo . . ."

"Tell him, goddammit! You want this town to go under?" His eyes swept the table. "While you belly up to the good booze and vittles." His words cut across the room like acid.

Calhoun said gently, "Clay, sit down, man."

He realized the good sense in that. His arm was pounding, his head throbbed. Seated, he looked around at the group. No one dared offer him food or drink.

"Well?" And when there was no response he said, "It is our last chance. I will ride out and tell Fahnstock if you are afraid."

"You should be in bed," Hollingsworth said severely. "You cannot even sit a horse."

"I sat a horse to get here, mister."

"Clay, be reasonable," Calhoun said.

"It is only you now who can stop the drive," Tanner said. "It is not too late."

"But what's to stop Fahnstock just bringing his herd in, even if he is told not to. I mean at this point?" said Butterfield.

"You are the council. A word from you men and the farmers will back you to the hilt. And you know the railroad isn't going to ship without your agreement."

There followed a pause in which Hollingsworth sighed at the far wall of the room. "Maybe." He brought his gaze onto the group at the table. "Maybe he is right, gentlemen. Maybe it would work. After all, it is never over till the shouting." And he added thoughtfully, "There is always time enough to die."

These words fell with a definite resonance in the room. Calhoun said, "It's crazy . . ." His eyes went to the clock on the wall. But it was Coy O'Donnell who spoke, looking at his own gold watch. "Noon," he said. "It is noon."

Clay Tanner heard it first. He was on his feet and out the door almost before the others caught it. At first it was like a distant busyness. They sat, transfixed by what each really knew it to be, as the sound increased; and they heard a man downstairs yell, "It's Fahnstock! The cattle are coming!" There was more shouting while the sound of the herd came closer—right into the room where the men at the table sat and looked at each other.

22

Tanner was oblivious to the pain in his arm as he ran down the steps to the street. It only flashed through his mind how amazing that in his weakened condition he was able to run at all. Then he saw Tom.

"Take my horse to the livery," he told the boy. "I got to find Sharkey. Where's your sister?"

"Back at Olsen's, I run out on her."

The street was deserted, yet filled now with the yells of the oncoming cowboys and the drumming and bawling of the Fahnstock herd. They were not running, but the sound of their gait took precedence over all else. A drop of water hit the back of Tanner's hand, and it was then he realized he had even forgotten the weather in the urgency of his purpose. At that same moment the sky darkened and the sun disappeared completely behind a wall of cloud.

Tanner said, "You get on back to Olsen's house yourself. You can cut through behind Main Street."

"You have got to come too," Tom insisted.

"I got to find Sharkey."

"But . . ." The boy was staring helplessly at Tanner.

"Stay with your sister," Tanner said then. "That's how you can help me. I am heading for the loading pens."

Tom's face was very white as he nodded.

Tanner leaned forward a little, and said again, "Take care of her." And he touched the boy's shoulder, urging him. As the din of the oncoming cattle herd grew.

The next moment lightning forked the black sky and a crack of thunder drove right across the town. The leaders of the herd broke wild-eyed down the street. The first ones were jogging now, still clearing the boardwalks and pillars that supported the canopies. But those crowding behind were not so nimble, and here and there a post was struck until finally one cracked under the weight of the herd.

But the cowboys were still in control, though their margin was a slim one. Fahnstock rode ahead with two other men, trying to slow the leaders. And in this way the herd broke toward the main part of town.

"They will stampede sure," shouted Tod Mallory, the trail boss, trying to be heard above the running cattle. "There is no stopping them now."

"We will turn them critters before they hit the pens," Fahnstock vowed.

Tanner, crossing the street, looked up, but though he could hear the rumble of the herd, it was still not in view, for they were coming off the trail at a right angle to the town.

He himself was still a long way from the loading pens. Stopping now outside the Silver Dollar, he ran his hand over his face, trying to collect himself. He was not thinking clearly, he knew. The thought came to him that he should have ridden the dun, but it was too late now. But why was he going to the pens anyway? The office would be better. His—Sharkey's—office. Sharkey would be there. He had to find Sharkey.

Out of the side of his eye he noted the passer-by who stopped in surprise to stare at him, and hurry on. Tanner did not look in his direction, for he knew he needed to save his strength from idle talk.

And would Sharkey be there? The thought stood suddenly in the center of his mind. Or would he be off someplace with his new deputy? Maybe they were both down by the loading pens?

And again he was swept with that strange feeling of mystery about Sharkey that he had known ever since he was a boy trying to talk to his mother about him. Why had she always avoided such talk? And himself, how did he feel? Why did he feel so mixed about that man? You couldn't but help sometimes liking him.

Suddenly Siringo was in his mind and he remembered what Hollingsworth had said about Sharkey topping the old wolf way back in the early days. A dizziness swept him then and the thought faded. God, he was tired. It would be good to find a place to lie down.

He began to walk down the boardwalk toward the office. Yes, too late for the quarantine to be enforced now. But they could keep the next herd out. And they could rein down Siringo. Himself and Sharkey could do it. Another wave of dizziness took him. Then, somehow from somewhere a fresh strength filled him and he stepped surely along the boardwalk. Yes, the marshal's office. There would be guns and ammo there.

All at once he was sure that he saw Sharkey crossing the street with a man, but he was too far away to raise a shout. As the sound of the Fahnstock herd bore closer.

23

Sharkey and Dutch Tommy crossed quickly to the bank. The sky had lightened somewhat.

"You got the horses in the alley, you got fresh mounts at Whistle Creek." Sharkey reviewed it to impress the plan on his deputy. "Give me two minutes to get to the back door. Then you go in the front."

Dutch Tommy nodded.

"Remember, they will already be nervous with the herd coming. They'll be closing the bank. Tell them to pull down the blinds. Lock the door. They'll do what you say. And be sure the alley door is open for me. They will do anything you want on account of that thing on your shirt there." Sharkey said it fast, in time with their pace as they crossed the street.

Now the first head of cattle broke into Main Street and as Sharkey saw them he began to whistle softly to himself. Them critters couldn't've come at a better time, he reflected, as he hurried into the alley that ran next to the bank.

Across the street in the marshal's office only a few yards north of the bank, Clay Tanner stood facing Siringo and three of his men. He had walked right into it. It had crossed his mind to follow Sharkey and his companion, but he had felt a sudden weakness again and had thought to sit down until his strength returned. And so he had gone to the office. Siringo and the others were there as though just waiting for him.

"You let my boys loose," the boss of the KT said.

"I do not have the keys," Tanner told him, the strength rising in him with a great force. "And if I did you wouldn't see them. You can go plumb to hell, Siringo. You are not taking over this town."

Siringo said nothing to that. He simply nodded to Hendry Swann, who walked into the next room and shot the lock right out of the cell door.

Across the street Sharkey heard the shots and he knew where they came from. It only figured natural that Siringo would be using the cattle to cover himself. Sharkey grinned. Same as he was doing. And he looked up the alley to make sure the horses were there.

When he entered the bank he found the two tellers loading the saddlebags he had given Dutch Tommy. Sharkey pointed his gun at Coy O'Donnell.

"We will open the other safe, Mr. Bank Manager," he said.

O'Donnell was already fuming at being duped by a deputy, and now seeing Sharkey he almost exploded in rage. "I might have known! I knew you could never trust a damn outlaw. Tanner is a fool. I have always said so!"

Sharkey looked at him coolly. "Get into that room and open the safe," he said. "And be quick about it." As they moved into the other room he said to Dutch, "Hurry it up."

When the other safe was empty and the sack he had provided was filled, he said to O'Donnell, "In there."

"You will not get away with this, Sharkey. There'll be a posse on your tail and they won't let loose till they've got you swinging from a cottonwood."

"Don't worry about it."

The other safe was cleaned out now, and Sharkey threw a rope to the man named Harvey, who was one of the two tellers. "You tie her," he said, nodding toward the girl, the other teller. He threw another rope to Dutch Tommy. "And him," nodding at Coy O'Donnell. "And the gags."

When O'Donnell and the girl were tied and gagged he told Harvey to turn around. The teller was very white in the face. He was a young man; probably this was his first job; and it was said that the girl was his fiancée. He looked now as though he wanted to fall, yet he was not without courage and so he took a grip on himself, and looked at his girl, trying to smile encouragingly.

Dutch Tommy was good at his craft. He had secured

the girl and O'Donnell in chairs. He stepped back, picking up the saddlebags.

Harvey had turned his back to Sharkey, as he'd been told to do; and now that desperado from another day took a soft step forward and brought the barrel of his Colt down on the back of the bank teller's head. Not too hard, but hard enough. Harvey slumped to the floor with a little cry.

"Done, by God," Sharkey whispered as he stood for a moment looking at the three of them and at the saddlebags and sack filled with money.

"We will cut now," he said to Dutch Tommy and they started to the back door.

He had just put his hand on the knob when there came a shout and a loud knocking on the door at the front of the bank. By now the cattle leaders had almost reached this part of town, yet the knocking and shouting could be heard above them.

"Marshal Sharkey! Are you in there? Tanner's been shot! Sharkey . . . Siringo has shot Clay Tanner!"

Sharkey did not hesitate. It was as though he heard the words only in the back of his mind. He pulled open the door and swept through with Dutch Tommy right on his heels. He was swearing then at the realization that somebody had seen him going into the bank. Or had they? Maybe they'd just seen him crossing with Dutch Tommy and had put two and two together, having seen the deputy enter. No matter. Only he cussed himself for not being more sharp.

He lashed the sack to the saddle horn and then mounted swiftly. As he brought his leg over the far side of the horse he heard the door of the bank crash open, and men shouting. Swiftly he turned the big bay Dutch Tommy had secured for the purpose, and dug heels into his sides. Dutch Tommy mounted with the saddle-bags across his horse's withers. And now the two raced in single file to the far end of the alley where it gave onto a deserted back street.

"Thought you said Tanner was out of it," Dutch Tommy said as they hesitated where the alley met the street, and then he spurred out into the open. And it was only at that moment that Sharkey heard the words that had been shouted at him through the bank door.

"Dutch." He dug his heels into the bay and as he drew alongside his companion he handed him the sack of money from O'Donnell's private safe. "The creek. I'll meet you." And he had turned his horse, Dutch Tommy's wild surprise etched into his own as he marveled at what he was doing instead of fleeing.

Then he was back at the alley and racing toward the street that was now a torrent of cattle.

Now the sky swiftly darkened and lightning slashed across the town followed by a tremendous crack of thunder. Rain began to beat down into the dust that was filling the air. The cattle ran harder now, stirring more dust, which would soon be mud.

Sharkey could not get through to the other side where he saw men entering the marshal's office. It must have been there, he figured. Tanner must have come to the office looking for him. Those shots. He remembered them now.

Then a gap appeared in the sea of cattle, it seemed

from nowhere, and he was in the middle of it, buffeted like a piece of loose cargo, hoping he would not catch a horn in his leg or in his horse. But he saw he was going to make it across. He knew he was going to make it. As men shouted and swore, and the cattle drummed toward the railhead.

The next thing he knew he was on his back in the street. But he had made it through. He scrambled out of the way of those razor hoofs and pulled up to his knees to fire at someone who was shooting at him from the marshal's office.

Suddenly he dropped his gun. It was his shoulder. Another bullet plowed into the street by his leg. And he was running and then rolling, rolling away from those bullets and hoofs, reaching for his other six-gun. Then he was on his knees.

And, by God, it was Siringo! He was right there, right in front of the office, on the boardwalk, his six-gun pointed right at Sharkey.

Siringo had lost his hat and his eyes were wild as he stared down at the kneeling, bleeding Sharkey. Siringo lost himself then; and Sharkey saw it in him. Siringo had him cold. Sharkey was still reaching with his good arm for his other six-gun and Siringo had him dead in his sights. But Siringo's weakness was greater; the pain of his humiliation at the hands of Sharkey those years long ago. "You bastard, Sharkey!" Those words were Siringo's final luxury.

And old Sharkey just did what was necessary. He simply moved. Swift as sound he drew his six-gun as the cattle swept behind him; and diving to his left, he fired. And his shot was true. He saw Siringo stagger. He fired again. Siringo fell like a blasted tree onto the boardwalk. But it was not the end.

From the roof of the building a rifle opened and Sharkey took it in the arm and shoulder that had already been hit. Then he was crawling. Another shot got him in the leg; this had come from the alley. God, he was boxed in their crossfire.

But he could still move. He rolled under the boardwalk as a blast of a shotgun just missed his head, spattering dirt into his face. Someone screamed and he thought he saw a body falling from the roof. Something landed with a great thud about six feet away in the street, but raising no dust for the rain was coming down hard now and mud had already formed. While the herd swept by and thunder cracked again across the black sky.

Another blast from a shotgun—he could hear better now—for the cattle were nearly past. And it seemed almost quiet now in the street with the cattle racing to the pens and Fahnstock's men trying vainly to turn them so they wouldn't stampede. Almost silent, save for the drilling hoofs as they receded, the driving rain, the scream of a man dying in the street, cut nearly in two by Clay Tanner's Greener .12 gauge.

It was Clay Tanner, upright on his own two feet, with his shotgun, his slinged arm, and carrying two more slugs from Siringo and Hendry Swann, who told the men to carry Sharkey into the Pastime.

"Got him, did I?"

Tanner nodded. "Right between the eyes."

"Not bad for a old-timer."

"Not bad for a new-timer neither," Tanner said. He stood looking down at Sharkey, who was lying on a pool table, while from his other side, Doc Hollingsworth investigated what was there. It didn't take him long.

"About it, Doc?" Sharkey's voice was weak but there was still grain in it. It was still his.

Hollingsworth's face was almost as gray as Sharkey's. "About it, Sharkey."

Sharkey let a gentle whistle of air come through his lips.

Tanner felt the dizziness hit him again. It had been all right during the action, but now standing quietly beside Sharkey it suddenly swept through him.

"Look like you need a drink." Sharkey's sudden voice hit him in surprise.

"Reckon I do," he said, straightening some. "How about yourself?"

"That is a dumb question."

Clay Tanner looked at Hollingsworth, who inclined his head slowly. There was a strange sort of smile on his face.

Sharkey almost choked on it, but he did revive some. Now his eyes opened a little more as he found Tanner again. "Son, you look like you oughta be lying here more'n me." He touched his lips with his tongue, trying to lick them. "Better drink yourn."

Tanner lifted the bottle. It went through him like a little fire, and he almost could not handle it; but then the warmth filled his entire body. It was good.

Hollingsworth said, "Why don't you sit down?"

Tanner didn't answer.

Suddenly Sharkey started to cuss a streak.

Tanner leaned over him. "Take it easy, oldtimer."

"What the hell d'you mean, take it easy!"

"Doc's doing all he can."

"Doin' all he can!"

Tanner looked helplessly at Hollingsworth.

"You'll be all right, Sharkey," Doc said. "I'll give you somethin' more for the pain."

At this Sharkey tried to raise up, but he was too

weak. Color filled his face, and now when the words came they were hard with anger.

"You horses' asses! I caught me a goddamn splinter in my thumb, must be big as a fence post . . . when I rolled under that boardwalk. Hurts like hell. What the hell d'you mean, take it easy; do somethin' about it!"

Tanner had to fight a sudden rise of laughter.

"You can dig it out, can't you, Doc?" Sharkey said.

"Sure can, Sharkey. Might hurt a little, though."

"Gimme another of that whiskey then so I can stand it." And Sharkey lowered one eyelid in a slow wink.

His voice was not strong now as he said, "Reckon we are even now, Marshal. Don't figure I would of got Siringo without you backin' me." The smile was weak, but it was there. "I am proud of you. Couldn't of done better myself, I don't mind sayin'."

Tanner had to lean close to hear what Sharkey said next. His words came just on his breath. But Tanner heard them.

"Know somethin' . . . maybe I did make my stake after all . . ." And then, even softer, but still Tanner heard it, "Son . . ."

His eyes closed then, but the jaw stayed firm. He didn't make a sound. This was how Sharkey died.

Looking at him Tanner noticed a loose button on Sharkey's shirt. It was hanging by a single thread. Without thinking anything, he reached down and pulled it off.

Hollingsworth was looking at the little splinter he had taken out of Sharkey's thumb. "He was a funny man," he said.

K16

When Annie and Tom Miller walked in, Tanner was going through Sharkey's pockets. When he came upon the little gold locket he knew whose picture he would find inside.

The undertaker came then. "A few customers for Boot Hill, eh, Marshal."

Tanner was looking down at the open locket which he held in the palm of his hand.

Without raising his eyes, he said, "He will not be buried in Boot Hill."

"Where then?"

"I will show you where."

He closed the locket. Then he leaned over and placed it carefully in the pocket of Sharkey's faded hickory shirt. He pulled down the pocket flap and buttoned it.

The rain was coming down harder when he walked out into the street. Clay Tanner didn't notice that to the east, above the mountains, the sky was clearing. He didn't notice that he was still holding the button he had pulled off Sharkey's shirt.